Sports Illustrated KIDS
GRAPHIC NOVELS

STONE ARCH BOOKS
a capstone imprint

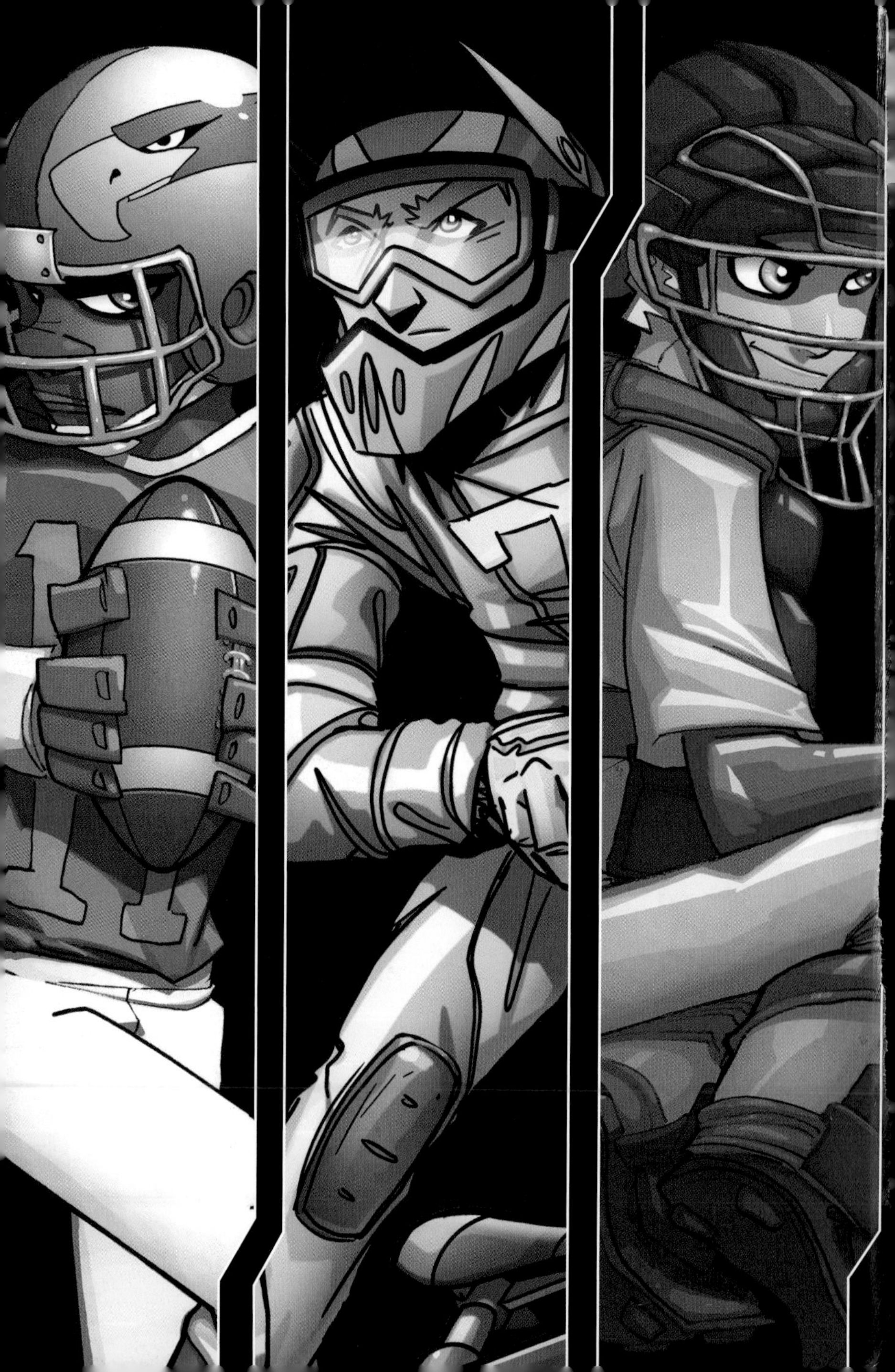

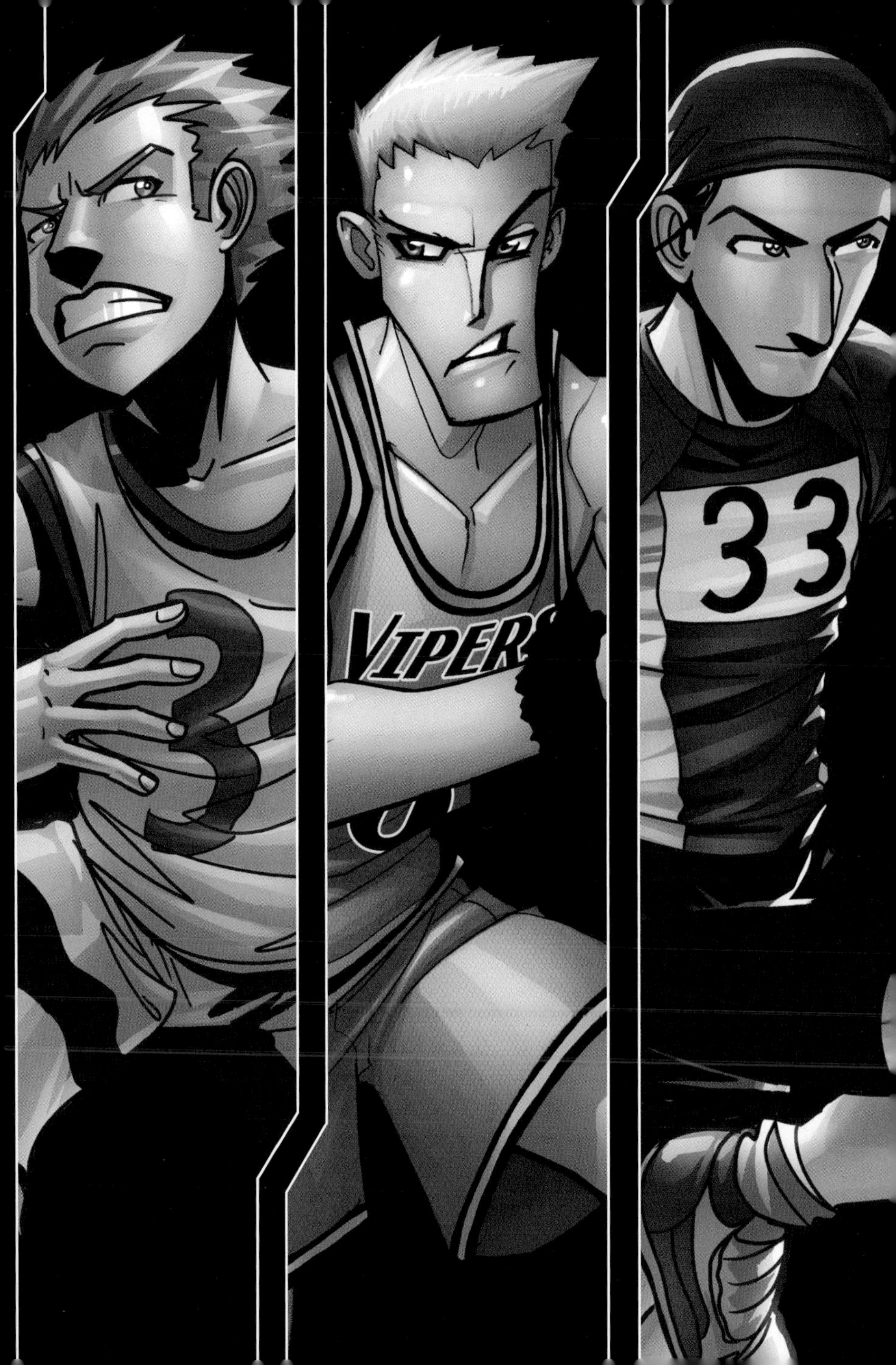
VIPERS
33

UP NEXT ›››

on Sports Illustrated KIDS

:02 SPORTS ZONE SPECIAL REPORT

:04 FEATURE PRESENTATION:

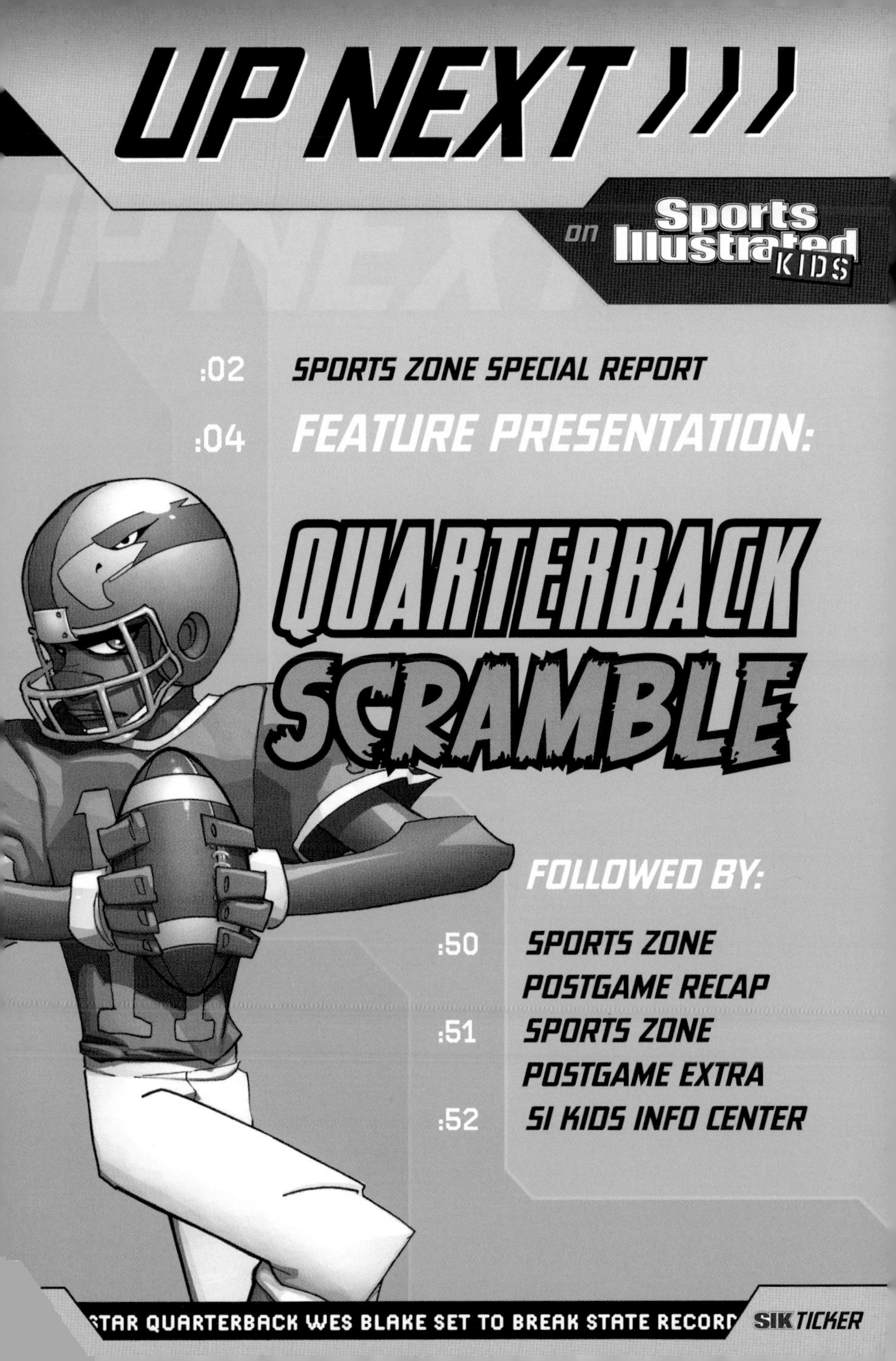

11

QUARTERBACK SCRAMBLE

FOLLOWED BY:

:50 SPORTS ZONE POSTGAME RECAP

:51 SPORTS ZONE POSTGAME EXTRA

:52 SI KIDS INFO CENTER

STAR QUARTERBACK WES BLAKE SET TO BREAK STATE RECORD SIKTICKER

SPORTS ZONE

SPECIAL REPORT

FBL
FOOTBALL

PNT
PAINTBALL

SOC
SOCCER

BSL
BASEBALL

BBL
BASKETBALL

HKY

TWO HAWKS QUARTERBACKS DON'T SEE EYE-TO-EYE AT ALL

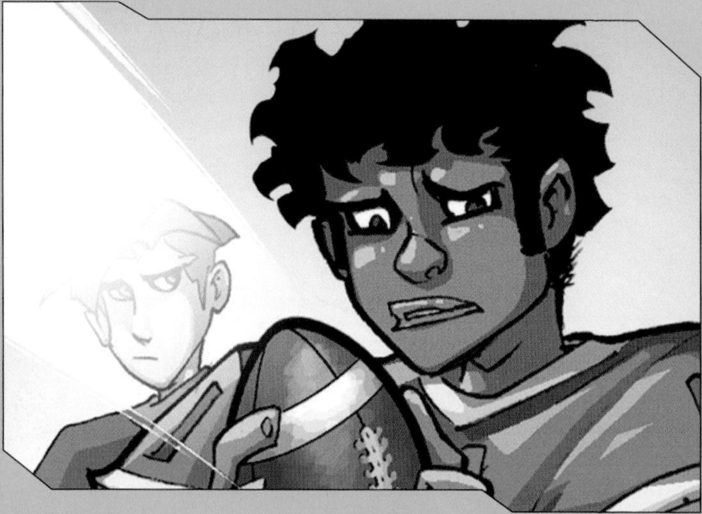

BEN PAULSON

STATS:
AGE: 14
POSITION: BACKUP QB

BIO: Ben Paulson doesn't mind being a benchwarmer. In fact, the very thought of stepping on the field to play quarterback makes him more than a little nervous. He's nothing like Wes Blake, who prefers to have the pressure placed squarely on his shoulders. However, rumors of Wes failing math class are making Ben more than a little worried about having to take over at quarterback.

Sports Illustrated KIDS

UP NEXT: QUARTERBACK SCRAMBLE

WES BLAKE

AGE: 14

POSITION: STARTING QB

BIO: Wes is the perfect team captain. He's confident, quick, strong, and a born leader. His math skills, on the other hand, need a lot of work. Algebra may not be very useful on the field, but in order to stay in the game, Wes will have to pass math class.

BLZ vs BHS
3-1
TGR vs RDR
33-32
EAG vs BAN
14-7
SPA vs WLD
4-3
BAN vs RDR
21-15
RZR vs LIG
4-3
BLZ vs BHS
3-1

SHELDON COOPER

AGE: 14

BIO: Sheldon is excitable, friendly, and outgoing. He is the color commentator for the Eagles' football team.

MARIA ALVAREZ

AGE: 14

BIO: Maria is calm, cool, and collected. She is the play-by-play announcer for the Hawks.

MRS. SINGER

AGE: 34

BIO: Mrs. Singer teaches math. She's honest and fair, but expects a lot out of her students.

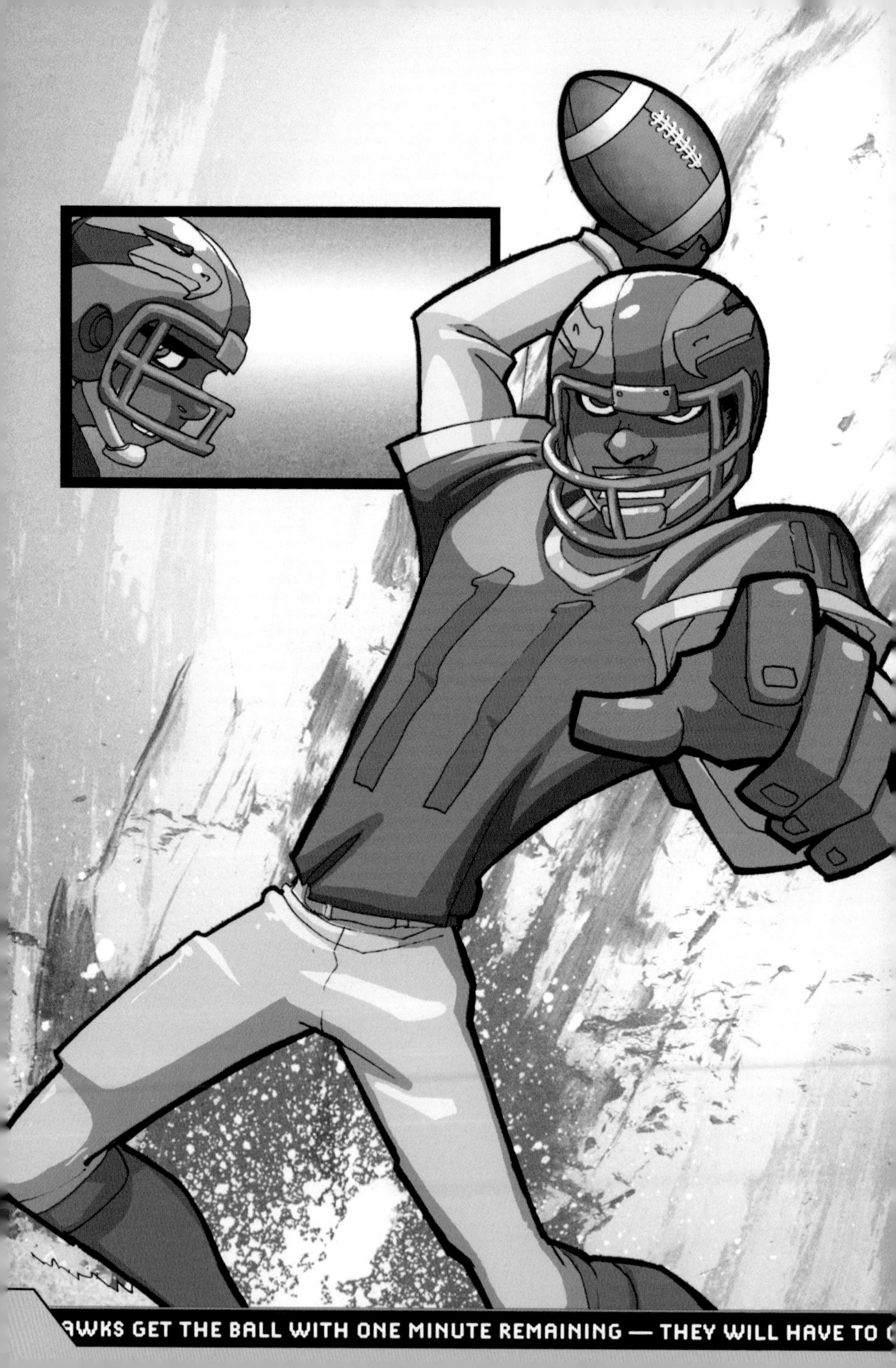
AWKS GET THE BALL WITH ONE MINUTE REMAINING — THEY WILL HAVE TO

Sports Illustrated KIDS

PRESENTS

QUARTERBACK SCRAMBLE

A PRODUCTION OF

STONE ARCH BOOKS
a capstone imprint

written by Brandon Terrell
illustrated by Gerardo Sandoval
colored by Benny Fuentes

designed and directed by Bob Lentz
edited by Sean Tulien
creative direction by Heather Kindseth
editorial management by Donald Lemke
editorial direction by Michael Dahl

Sports Illustrated KIDS *Quarterback Scramble* is published by Stone Arch Books,
1710 Roe Crest Drive, North Mankato, Minnesota 56003.
www.capstonepub.com

Printed in the United States of America in North Mankato, MInnesota.
052019 000080

Summary: Ben is happy to ride the bench — until the Hawks' star QB, Wes, gets suspended for pulling poor grades in math. With Ben at the helm, the offense stalls, and his teammates place the blame on his shoulders. Soon after, a possible solution to Ben's passing problems reveals itself — but he's not so sure it's the right answer.

Library of Congress Cataloging-in-Publication Data
Terrell, Brandon, 1978-
Quarterback scramble / written by Brandon Terrell ; illustrated by Gerardo Sandoval and Benny Fuentes.
p. cm. -- (Sports Illustrated kids graphic novels)
ISBN 978-1-4342-2220-6 (library binding)
ISBN 978-1-4342-3070-6 (paperback)
ISBN 978-1-4342-4952-4 (e-book)
1. Graphic novels. [1. Graphic novels. 2. Football--Fiction. 3. Self-confidence--Fiction.] I. Sandoval, Gerardo, ill. II. Fuentes, Benny, ill. III. Title.
PZ7.7.T46Qu 2011
741.5'973--dc22 2010032920

30 YARDS WITH NO TIMEOUTS LEFT TO HAVE ANY CHANCE OF BEATIN SIK TICKER

This is it, Maria! Wes Blake is one touchdown away from another amazing win!
That's right, Sheldon.
The Hawks' star quarterback has marched down the field with less than a minute left on the clock.
Some people are born leaders.
They're calm under pressure.
Calvin, I'm looking for you on this one.
Got it!
If the Hawks don't find the end zone here, the game is over.
This is too much, Maria! I can't look!

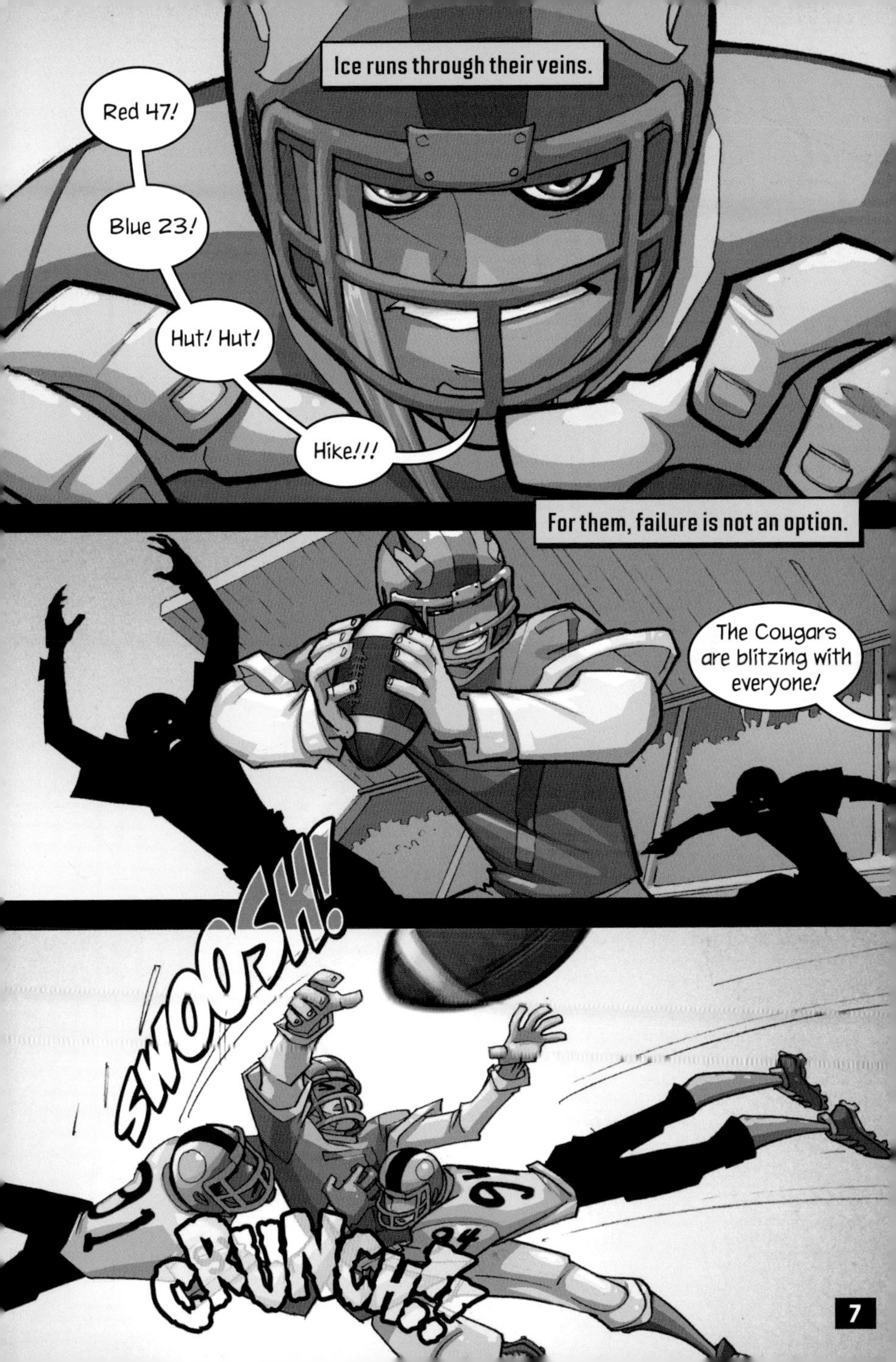
Ice runs through their veins.
Red 47!
Blue 23!
Hut! Hut!
Hike!!!
For them, failure is not an option.
The Cougars are blitzing with everyone!
SWOOSH!
CRUNCH!

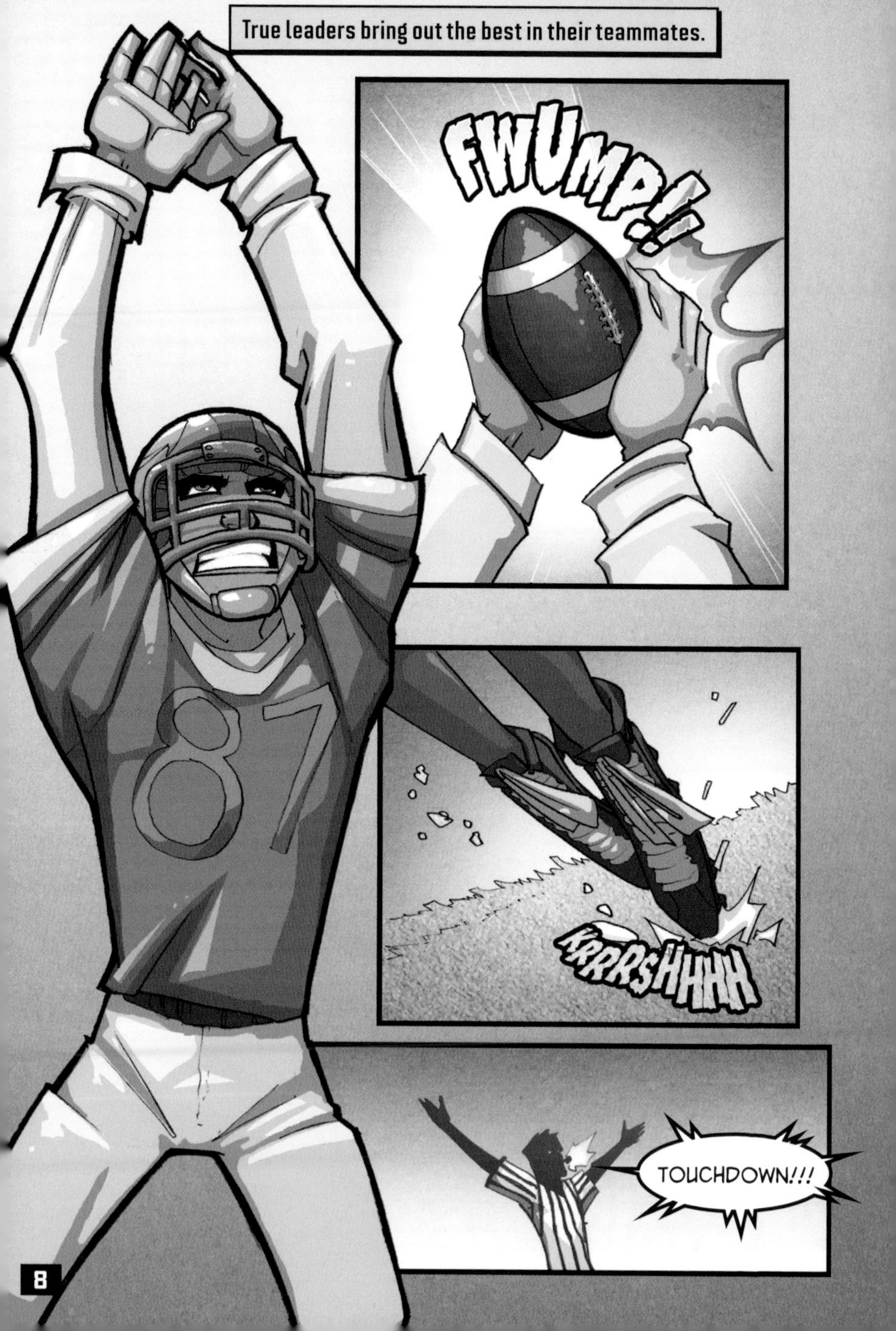
True leaders bring out the best in their teammates.
FWUMP!!
KRRRSHHHH
TOUCHDOWN!!!

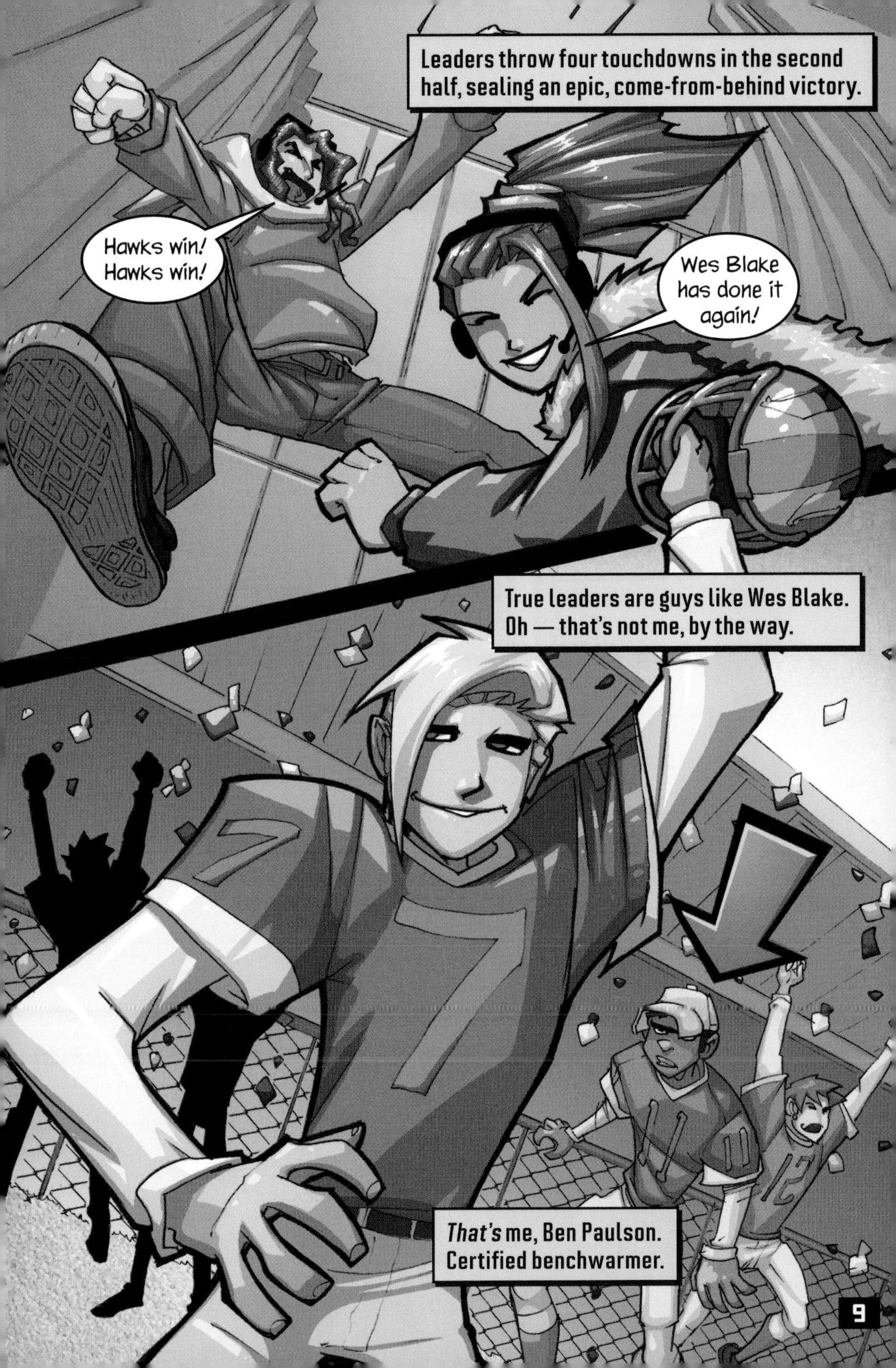
Leaders throw four touchdowns in the second half, sealing an epic, come-from-behind victory.
Hawks win! Hawks win!
Wes Blake has done it again!
True leaders are guys like Wes Blake. Oh — that's not me, by the way.
That's me, Ben Paulson. Certified benchwarmer.

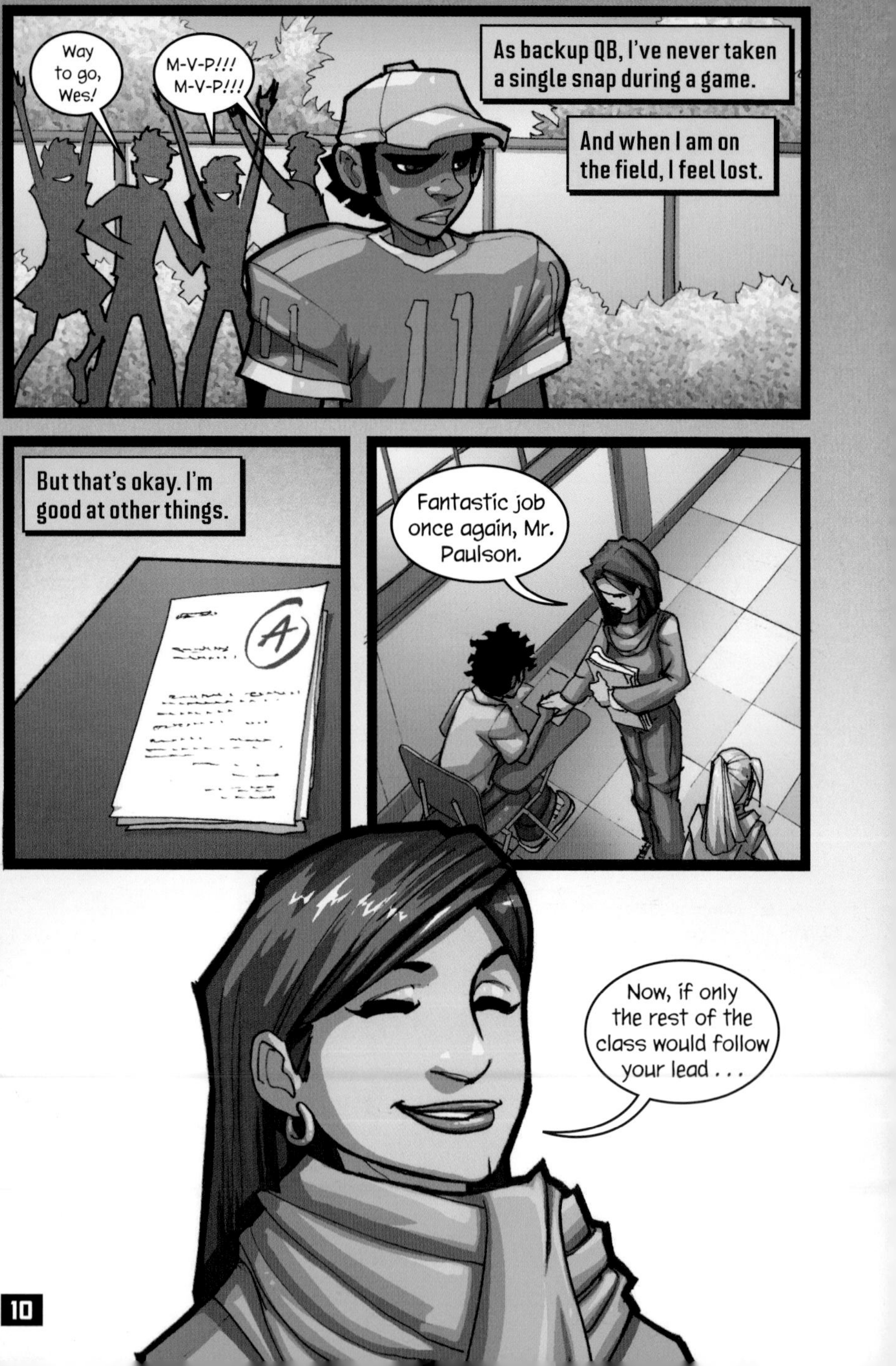
Way to go, Wes!
M-V-P!!! M-V-P!!!
As backup QB, I've never taken a single snap during a game.
And when I am on the field, I feel lost.
But that's okay. I'm good at other things.
Fantastic job once again, Mr. Paulson.
Now, if only the rest of the class would follow your lead . . .

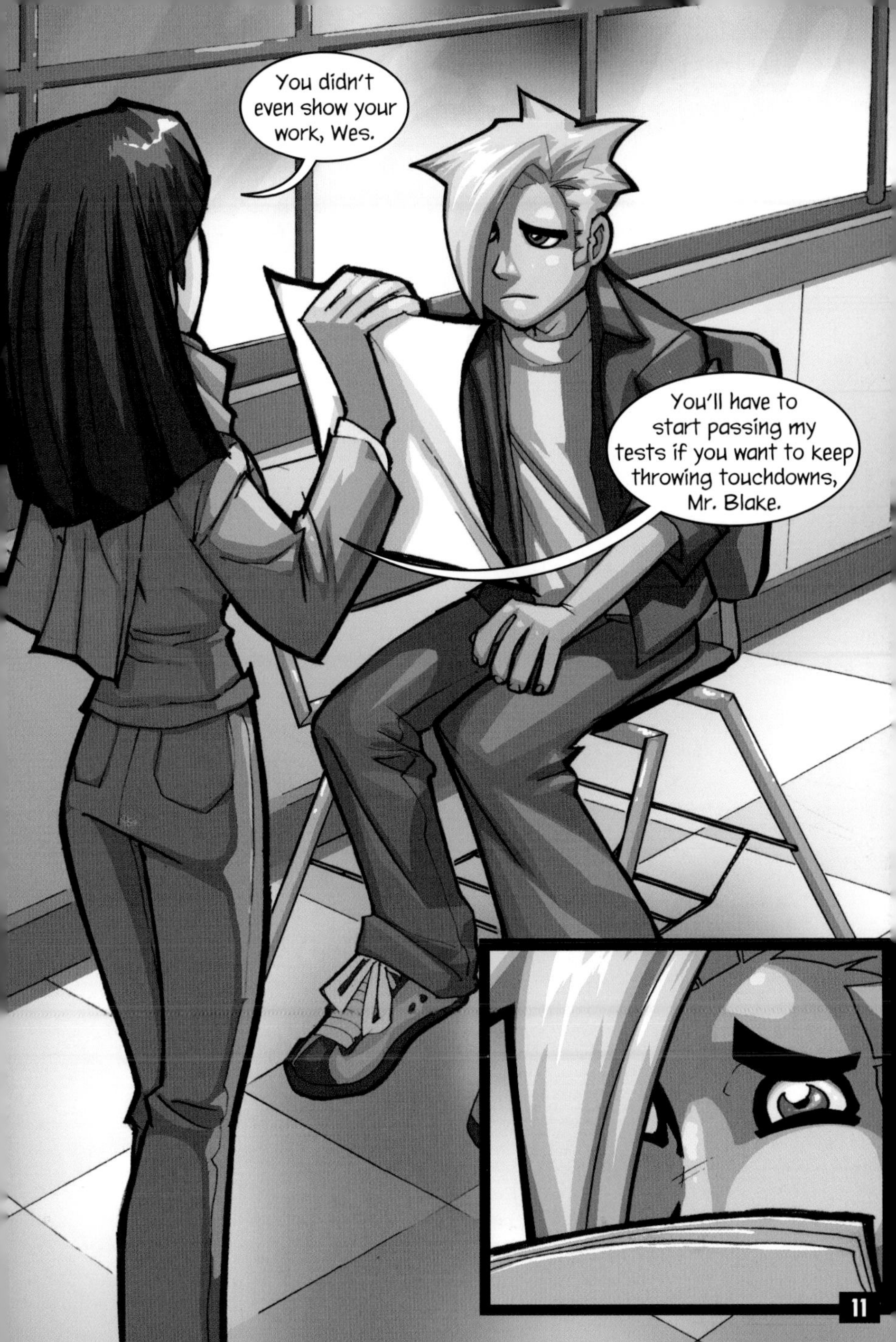
You didn't even show your work, Wes.
You'll have to start passing my tests if you want to keep throwing touchdowns, Mr. Blake.

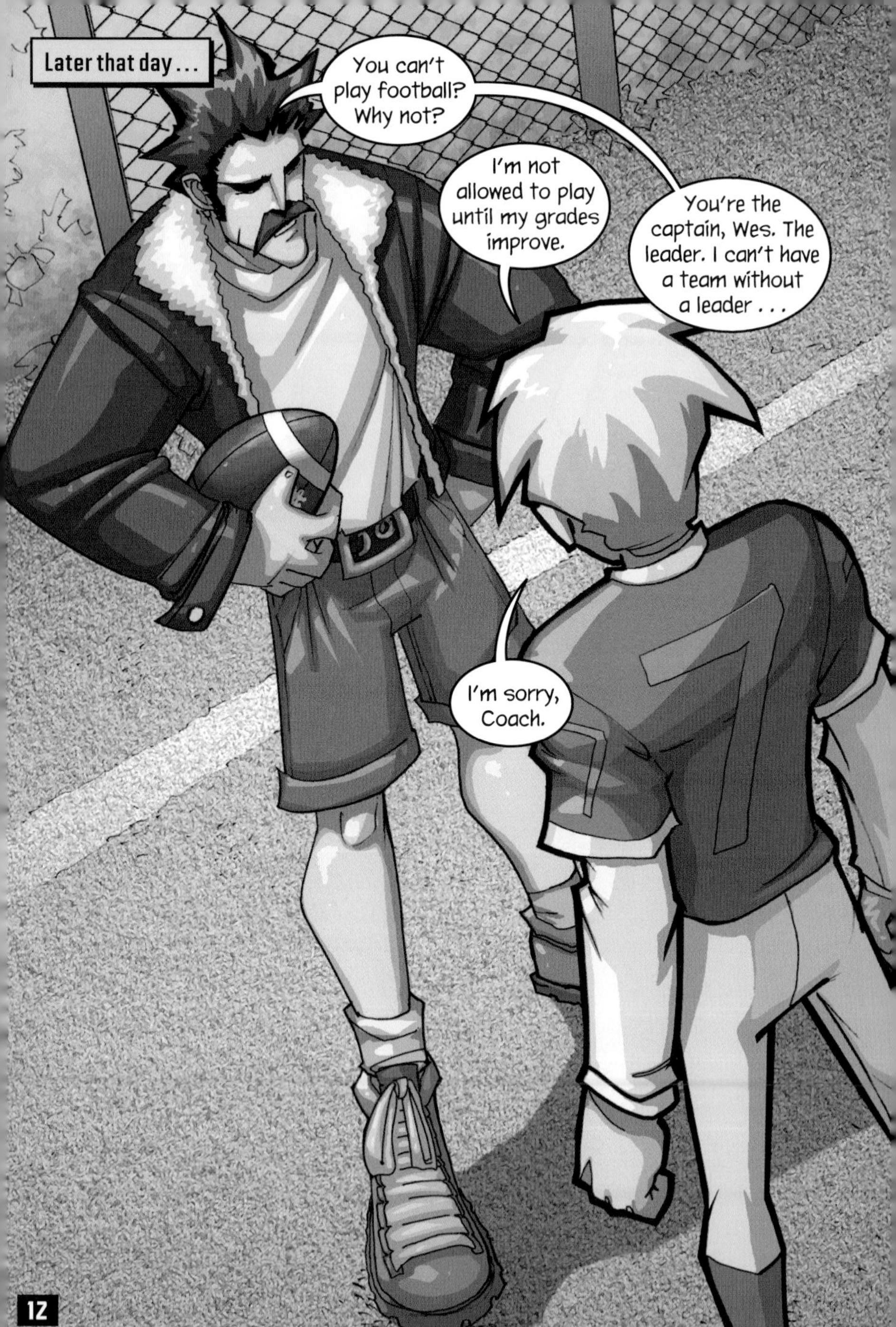
Later that day . . .
You can't play football? Why not?
I'm not allowed to play until my grades improve.
You're the captain, Wes. The leader. I can't have a team without a leader . . .
I'm sorry, Coach.

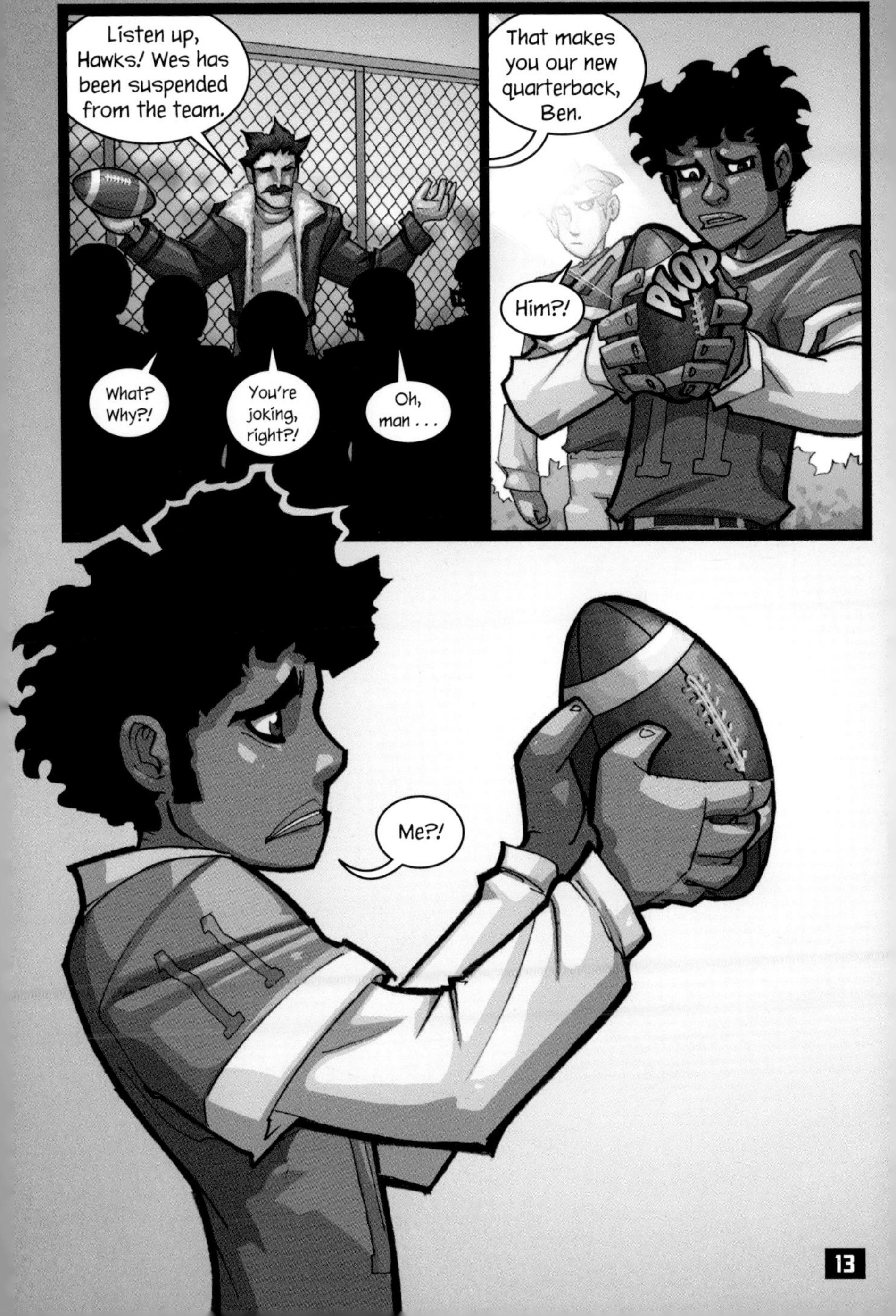

Listen up, Hawks! Wes has been suspended from the team.
What? Why?!
You're joking, right?!
Oh, man . . .
That makes you our new quarterback, Ben.
PLOP
Him?!
Me?!

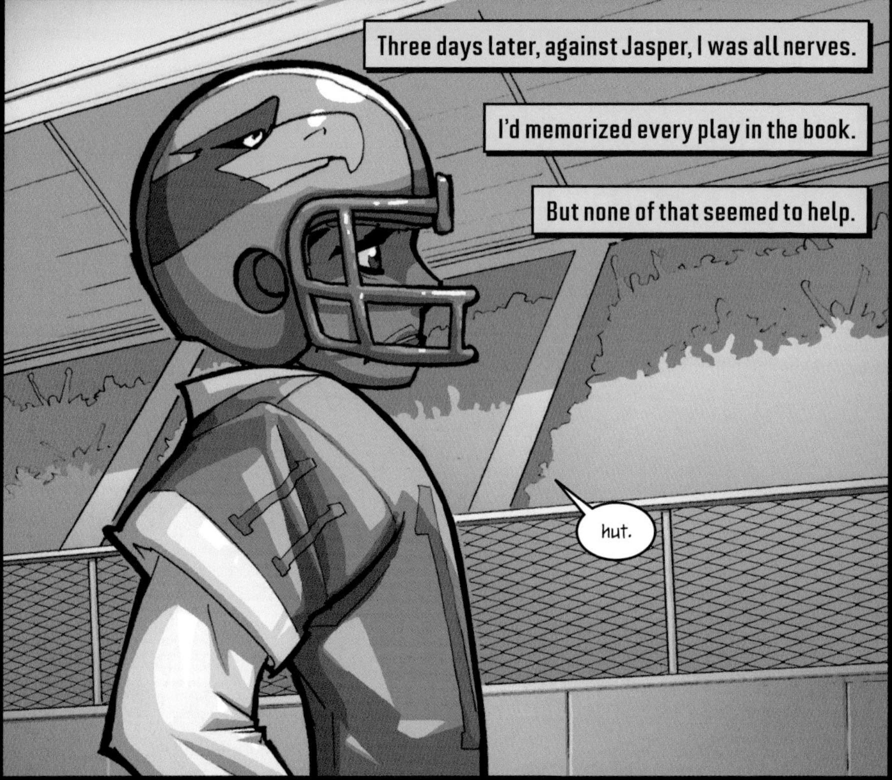
Three days later, against Jasper, I was all nerves.
I'd memorized every play in the book.
But none of that seemed to help.
hut.

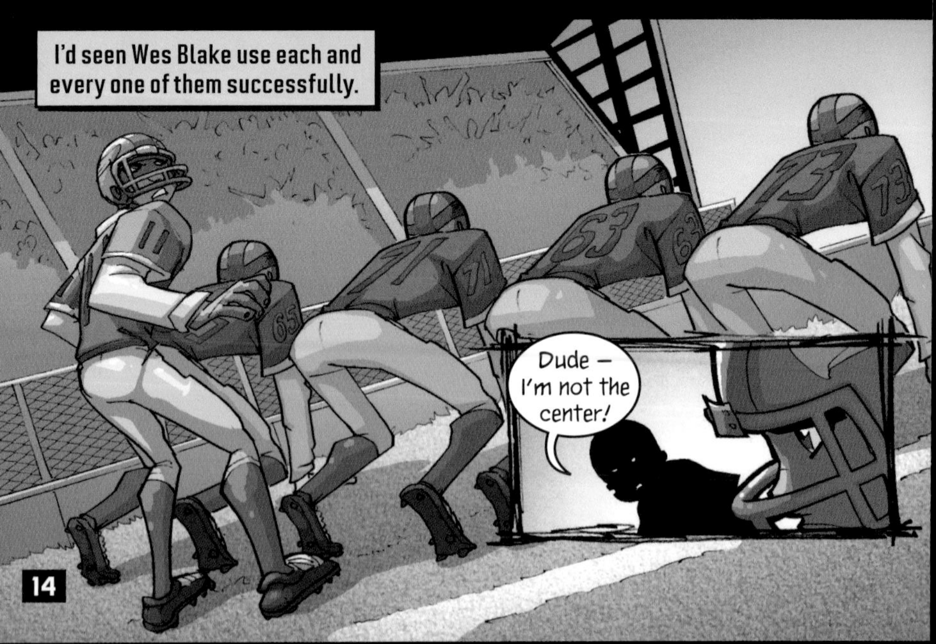
I'd seen Wes Blake use each and every one of them successfully.
Dude — I'm not the center!

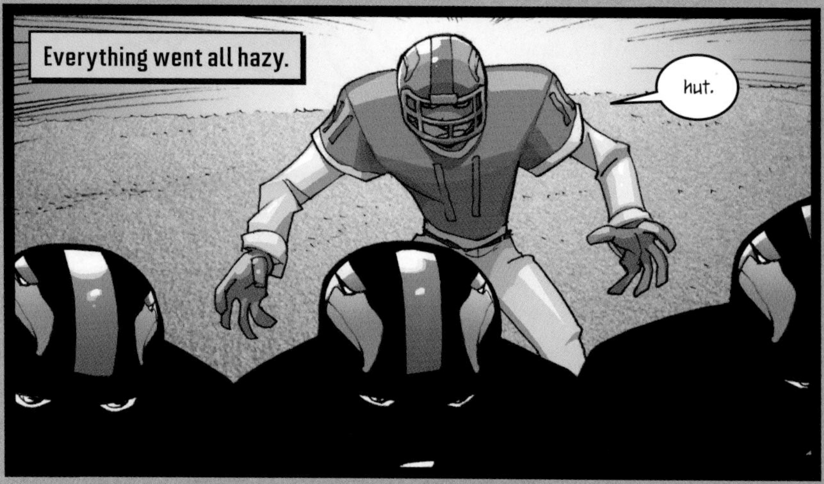
Everything went all hazy.
hut.

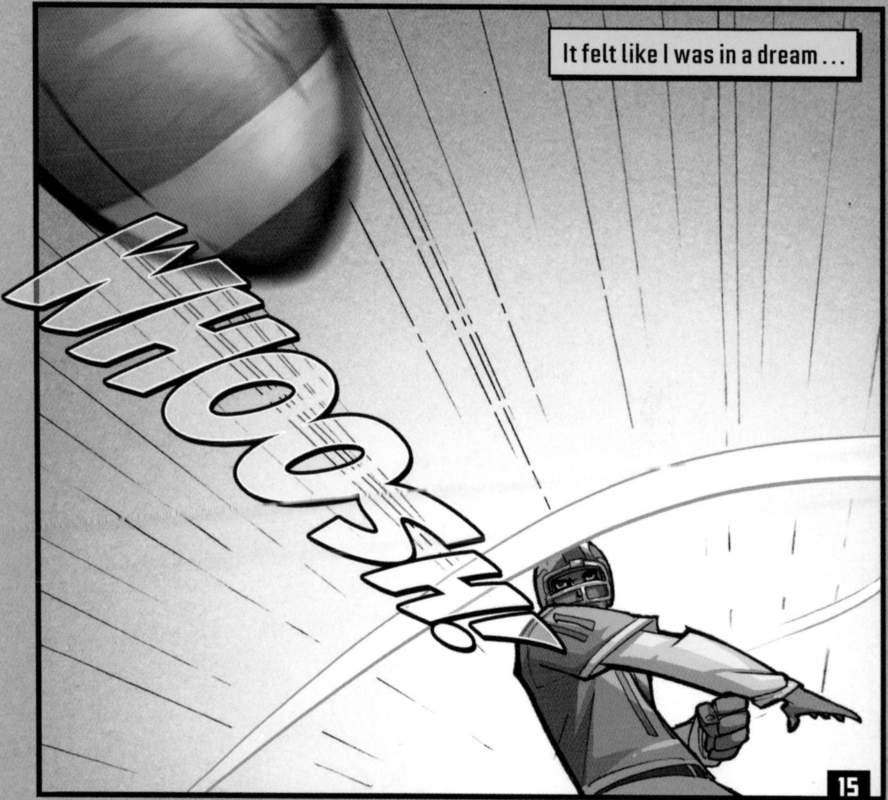
It felt like I was in a dream . . .
WHOOSH!

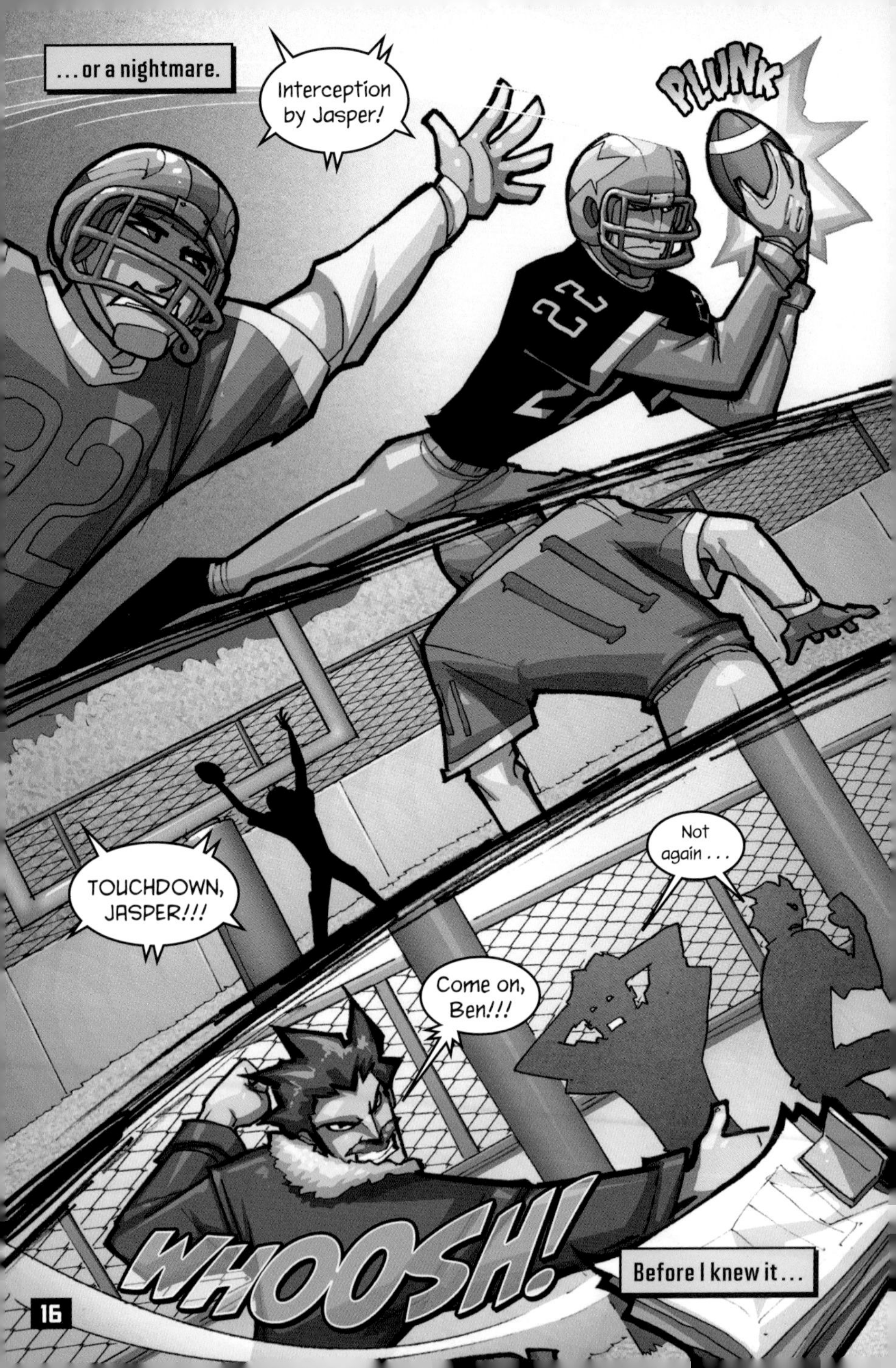

. . . or a nightmare.
Interception by Jasper!
PLUNK
TOUCHDOWN, JASPER!!!
Not again . . .
Come on, Ben!!!
WHOOSH!
Before I knew it . . .

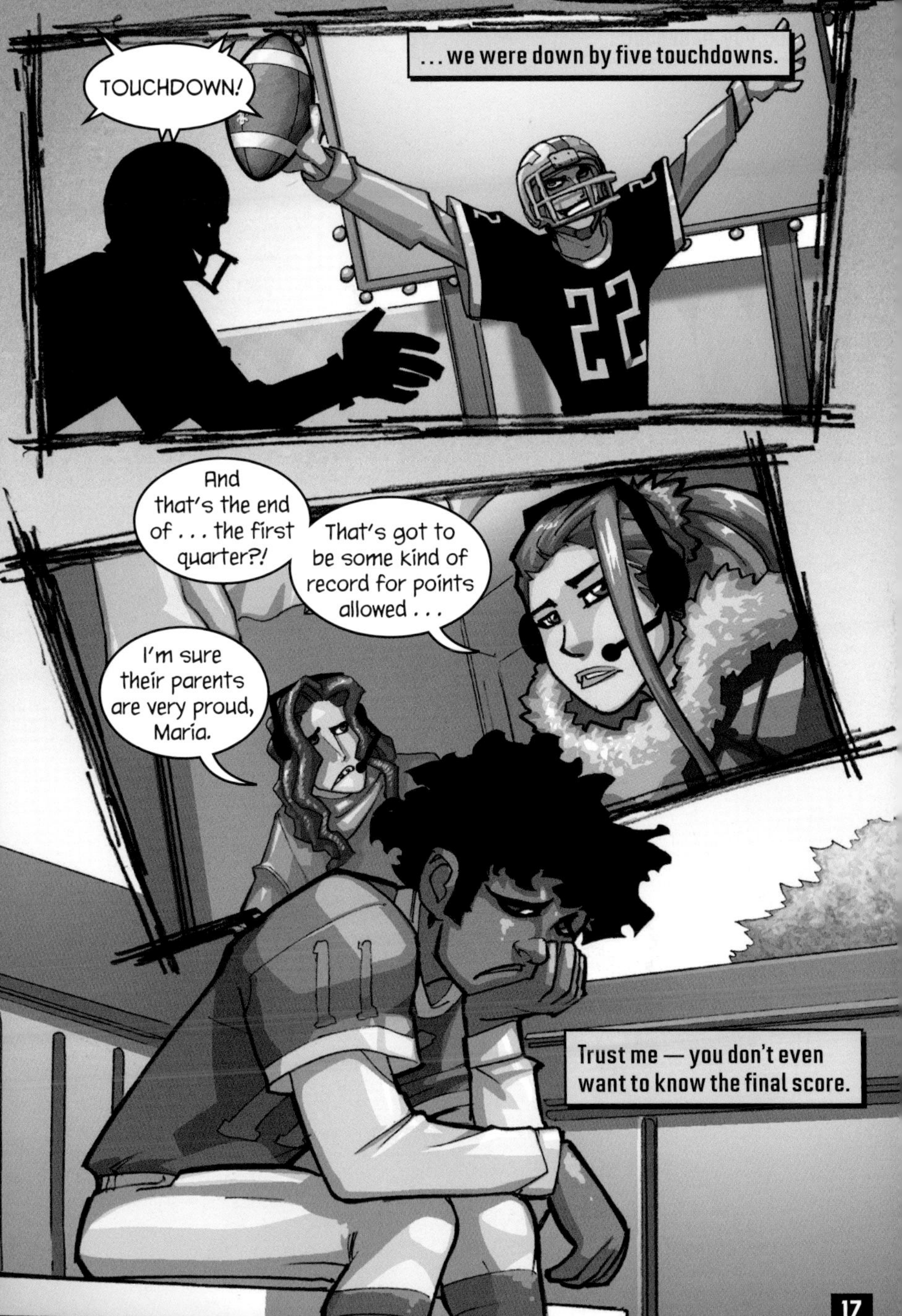

. . . we were down by five touchdowns.
TOUCHDOWN!
And that's the end of . . . the first quarter?!
That's got to be some kind of record for points allowed . . .
I'm sure their parents are very proud, Maria.
Trust me — you don't even want to know the final score.

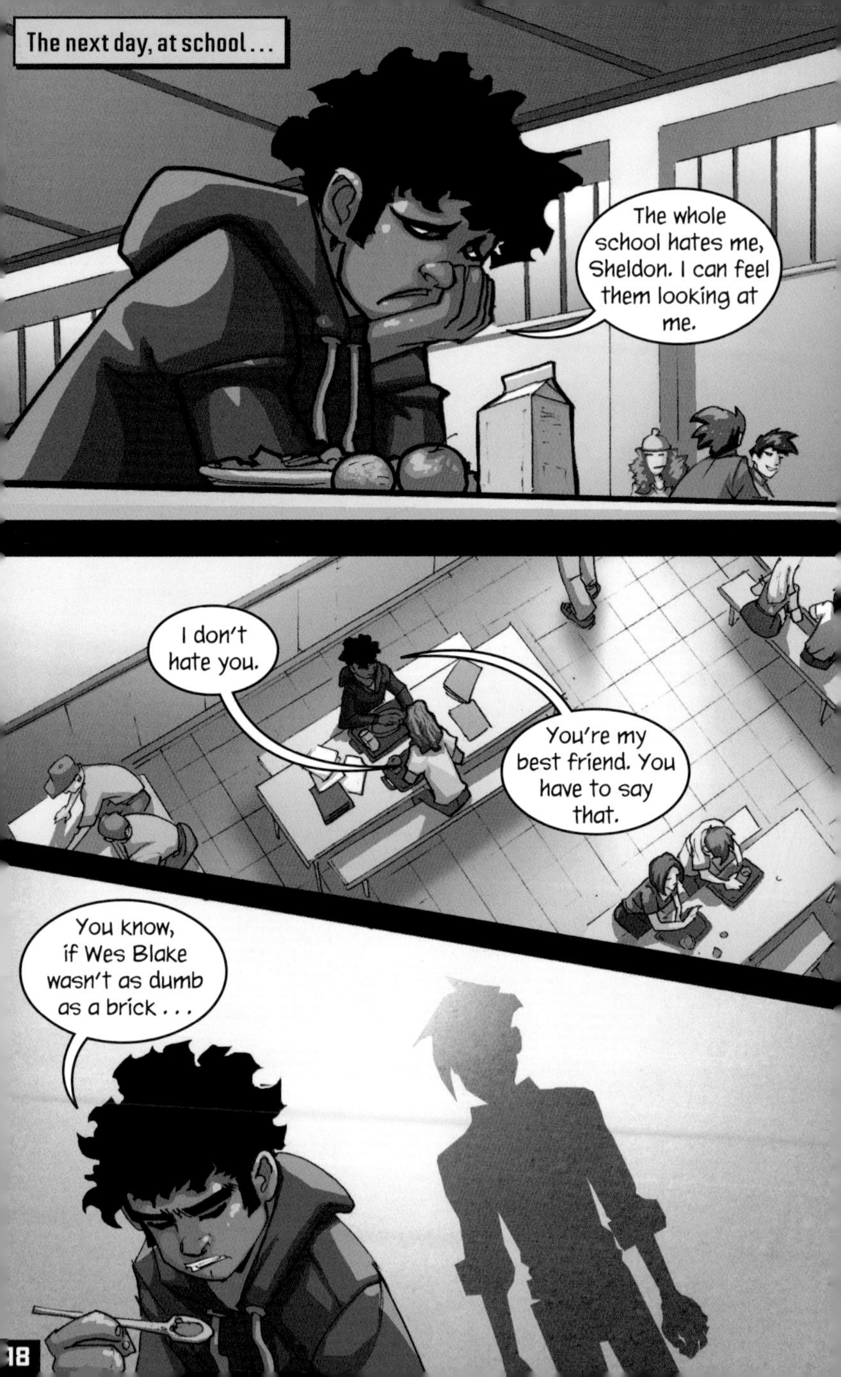

The next day, at school . . .
The whole school hates me, Sheldon. I can feel them looking at me.
I don't hate you.
You're my best friend. You have to say that.
You know, if Wes Blake wasn't as dumb as a brick . . .

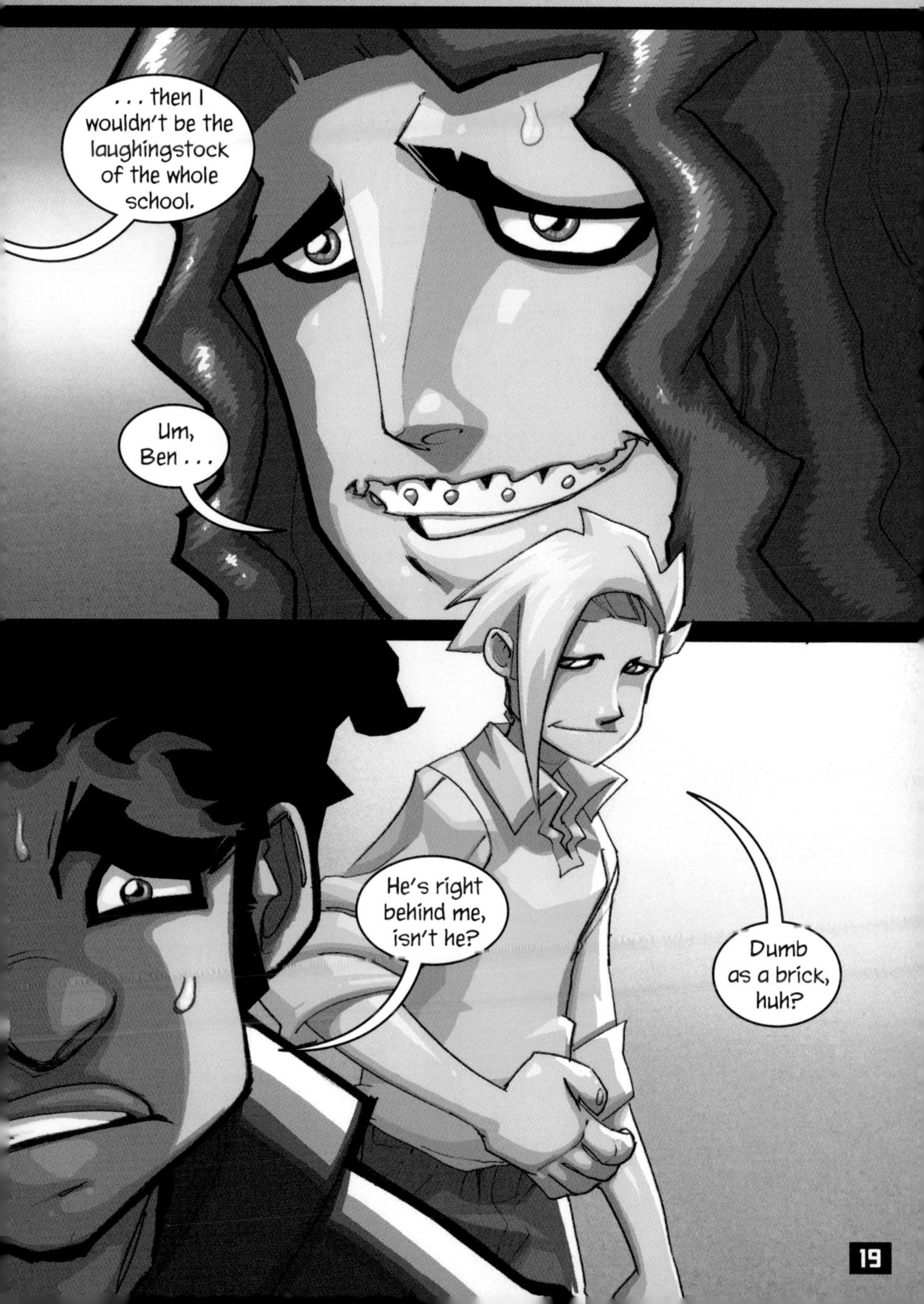
. . . then I wouldn't be the laughingstock of the whole school.
Um, Ben . . .
He's right behind me, isn't he?
Dumb as a brick, huh?

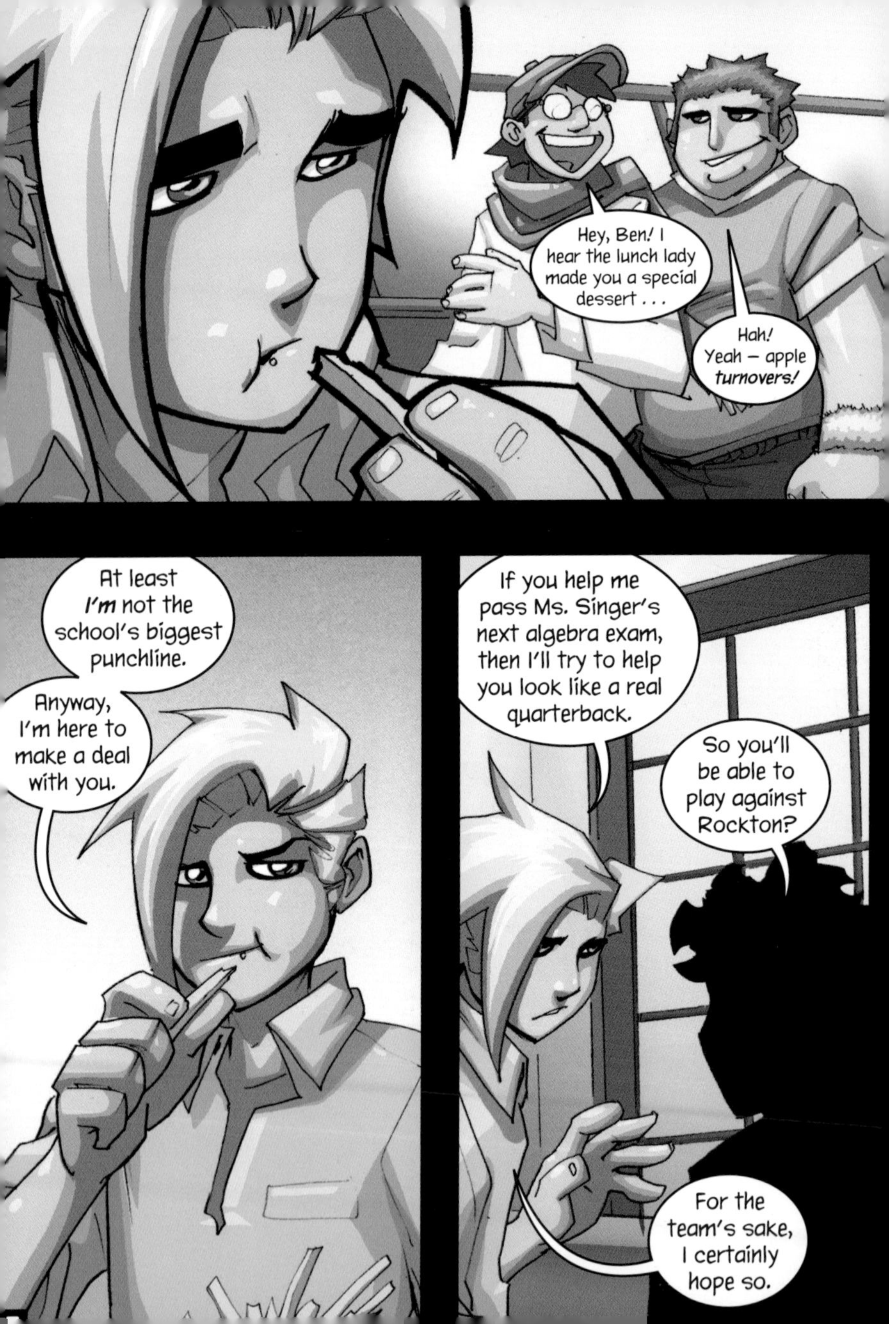
Hey, Ben! I hear the lunch lady made you a special dessert . . .
Hah! Yeah – apple *turnovers!*
At least *I'm* not the school's biggest punchline.
Anyway, I'm here to make a deal with you.
If you help me pass Ms. Singer's next algebra exam, then I'll try to help you look like a real quarterback.
So you'll be able to play against Rockton?
For the team's sake, I certainly hope so.

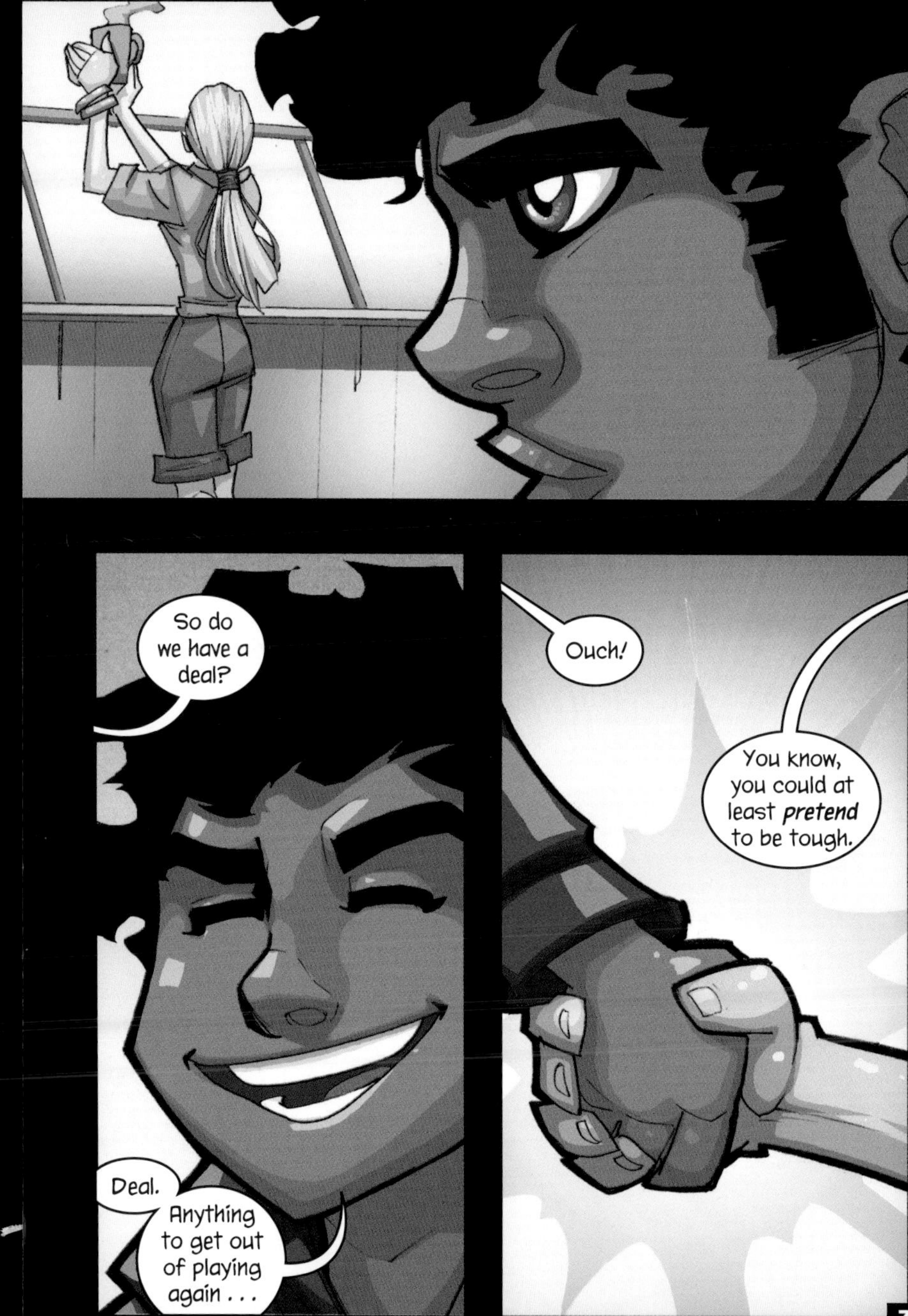

So do we have a deal?
Deal.
Anything to get out of playing again . . .
Ouch!
You know, you could at least *pretend* to be tough.

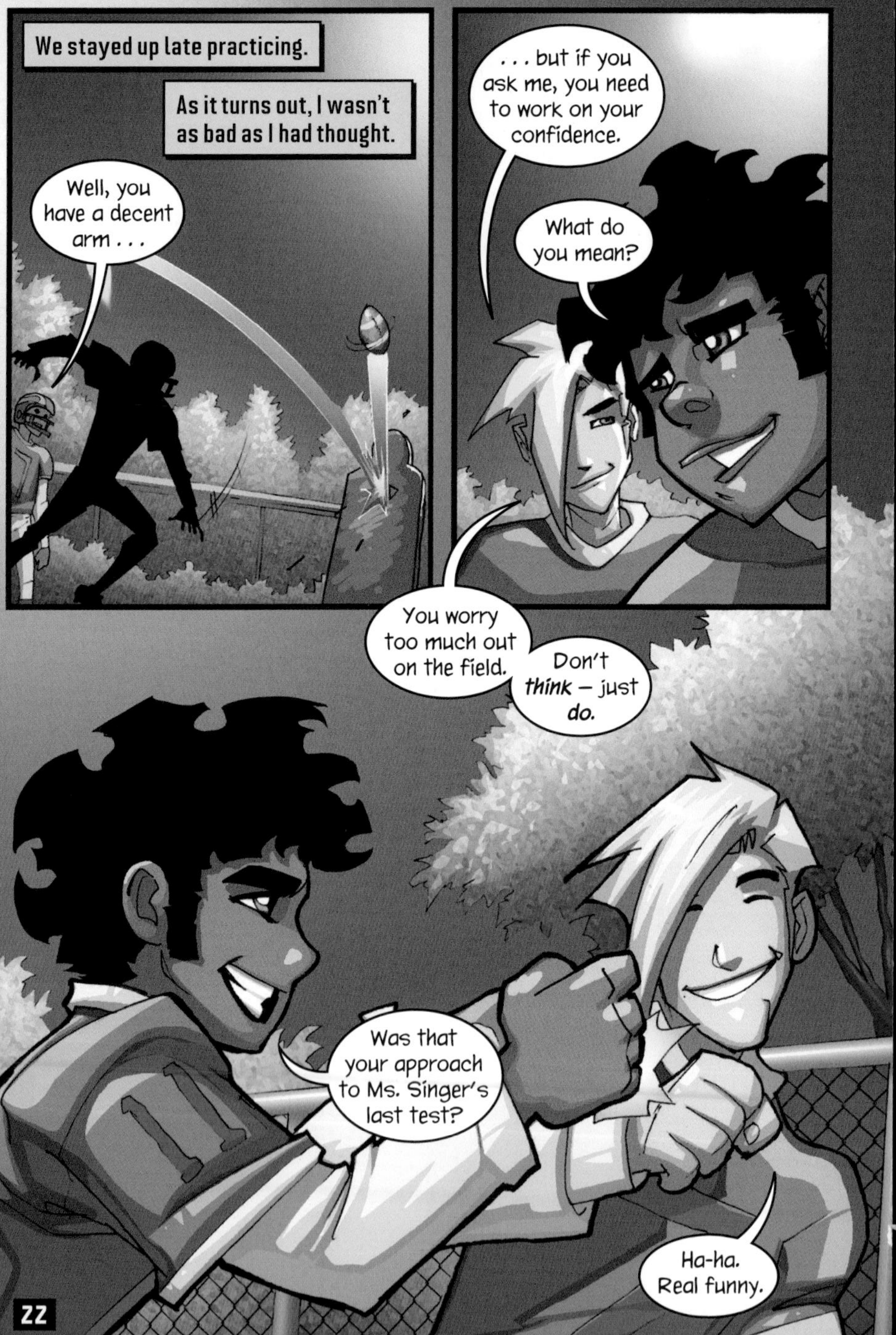

We stayed up late practicing.
As it turns out, I wasn't as bad as I had thought.
Well, you have a decent arm . . .
. . . but if you ask me, you need to work on your confidence.
What do you mean?
You worry too much out on the field.
Don't *think* – just *do.*
Was that your approach to Ms. Singer's last test?
Ha-ha. Real funny.

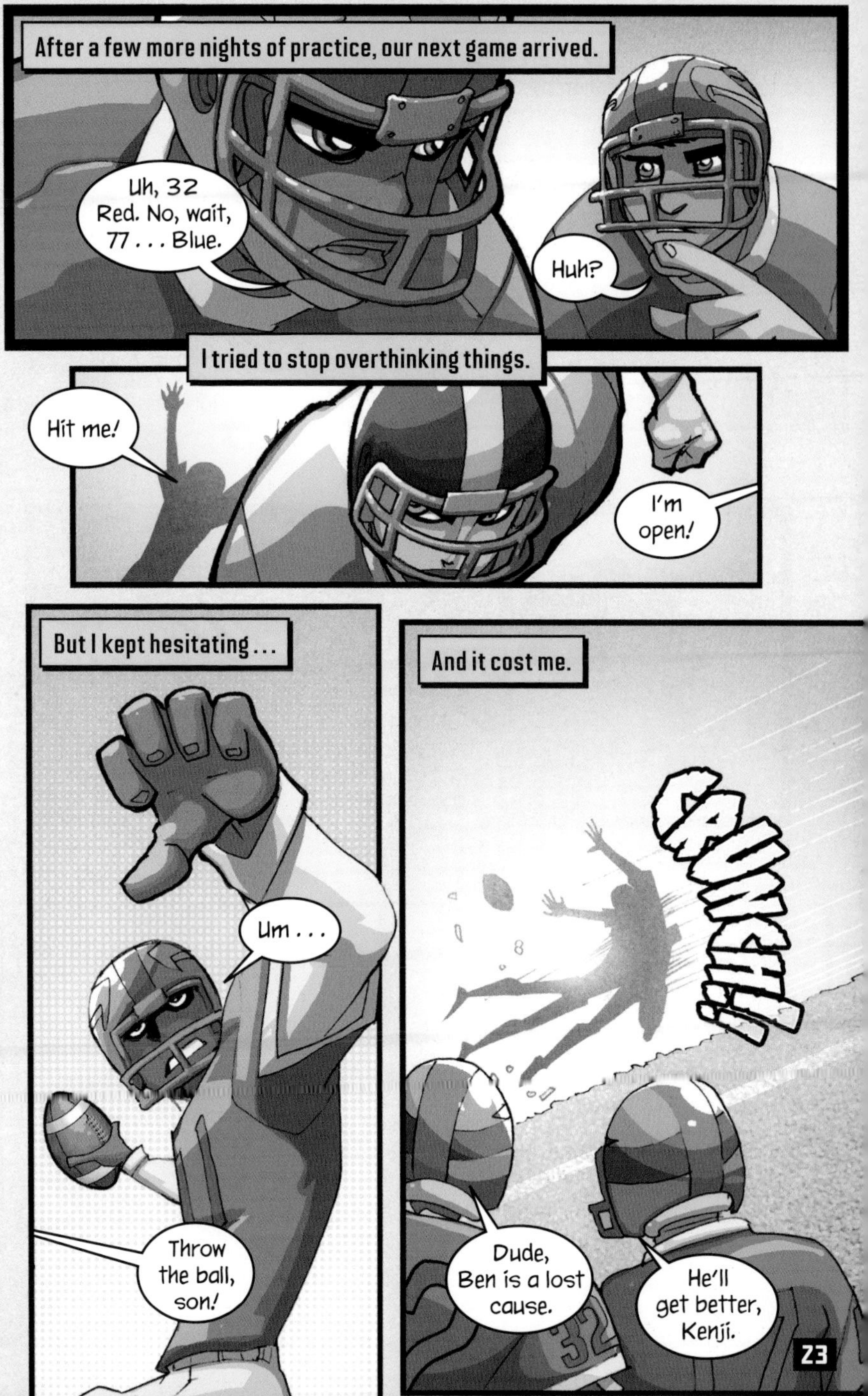

After a few more nights of practice, our next game arrived.
Uh, 32 Red. No, wait, 77 . . . Blue.
Huh?
I tried to stop overthinking things.
Hit me!
I'm open!
But I kept hesitating . . .
Um . . .
Throw the ball, son!
And it cost me.
CRUNCH!!
Dude, Ben is a lost cause.
He'll get better, Kenji.

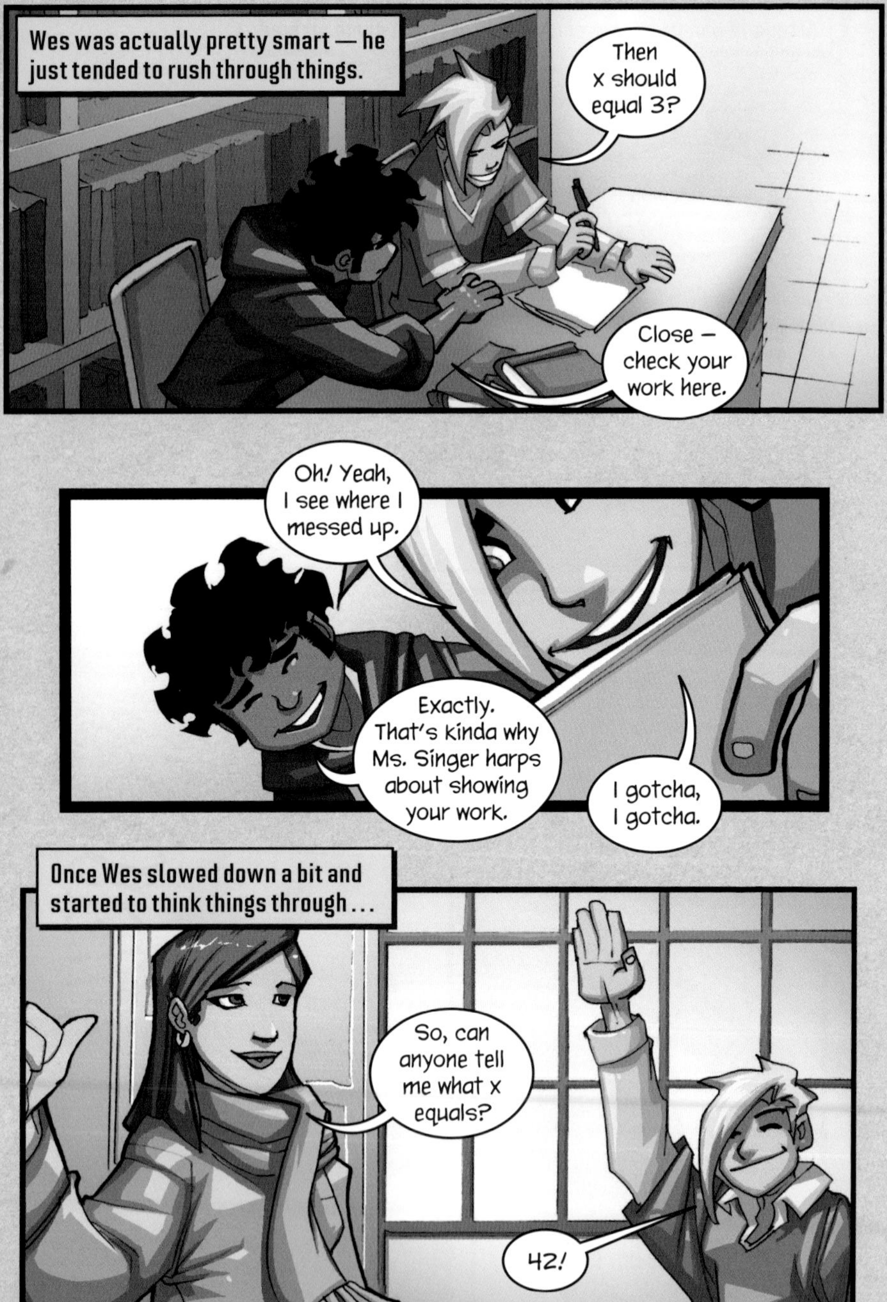
Wes was actually pretty smart — he just tended to rush through things.
Then x should equal 3?
Close — check your work here.
Oh! Yeah, I see where I messed up.
Exactly. That's kinda why Ms. Singer harps about showing your work.
I gotcha, I gotcha.
Once Wes slowed down a bit and started to think things through . . .
So, can anyone tell me what x equals?
42!

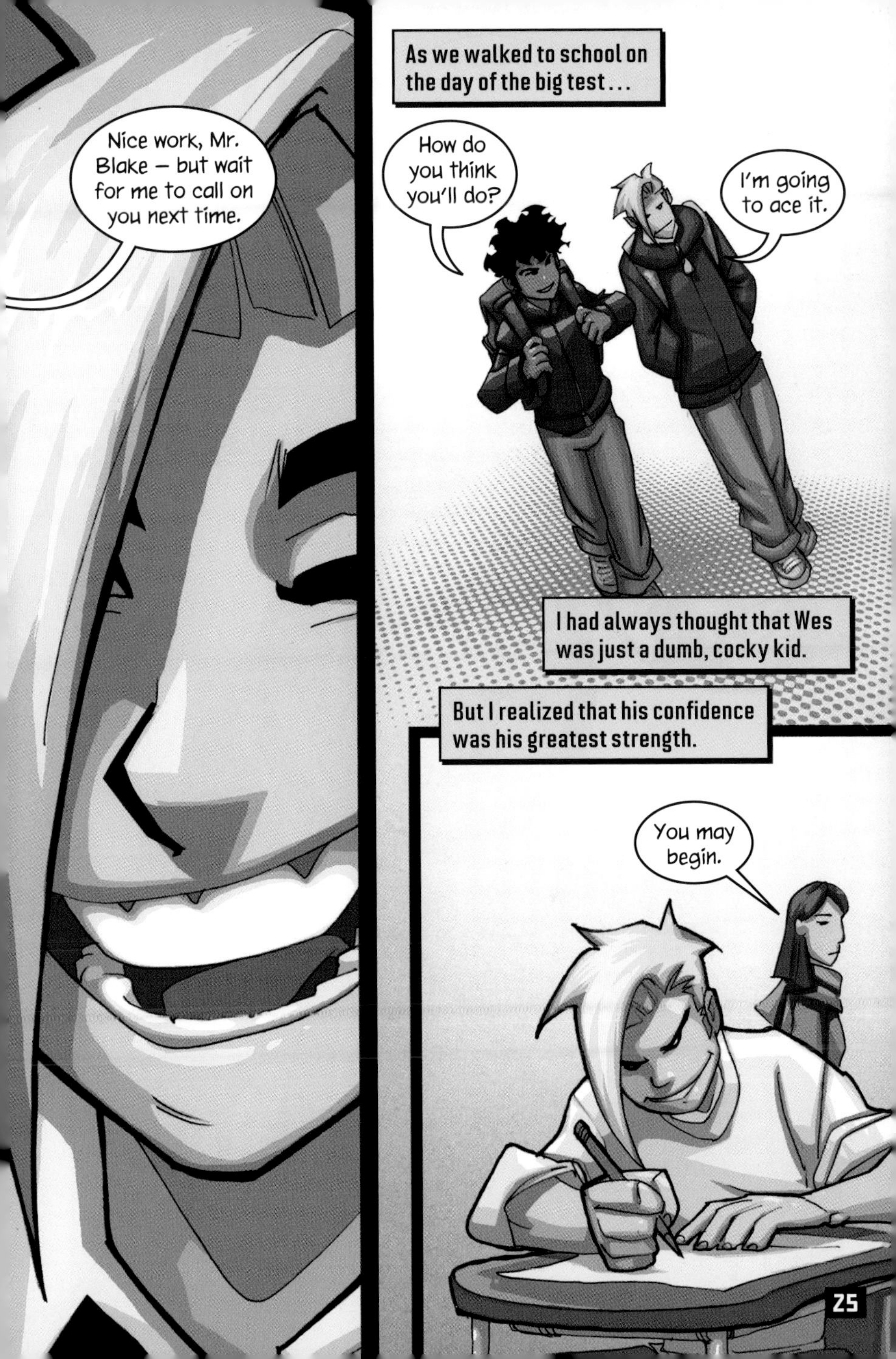
Nice work, Mr. Blake — but wait for me to call on you next time.
As we walked to school on the day of the big test . . .
How do you think you'll do?
I'm going to ace it.
I had always thought that Wes was just a dumb, cocky kid.
But I realized that his confidence was his greatest strength.
You may begin.

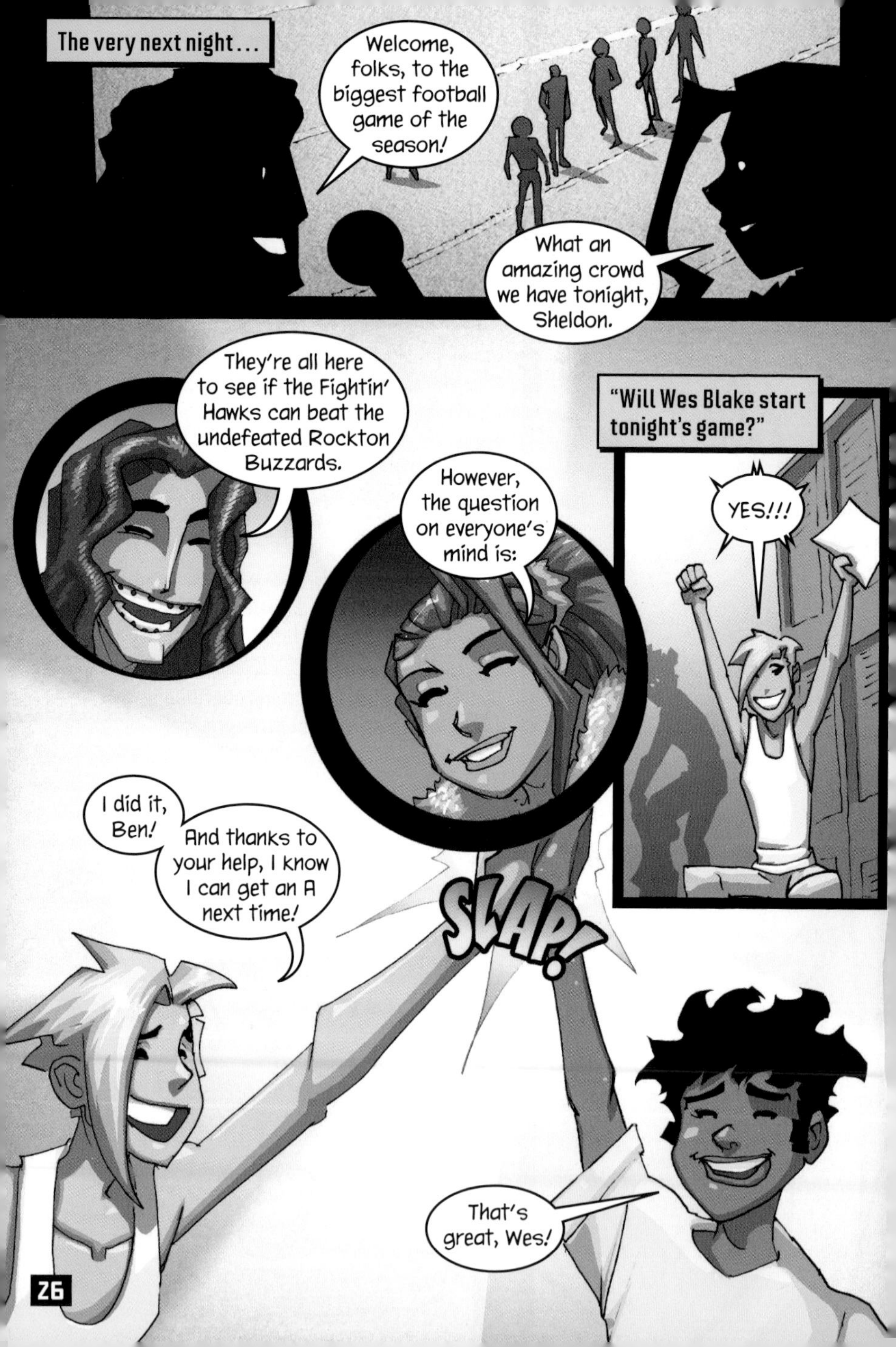
The very next night...
Welcome, folks, to the biggest football game of the season!
What an amazing crowd we have tonight, Sheldon.
They're all here to see if the Fightin' Hawks can beat the undefeated Rockton Buzzards.
However, the question on everyone's mind is:
"Will Wes Blake start tonight's game?"
YES!!!
I did it, Ben!
And thanks to your help, I know I can get an A next time!
SLAP!
That's great, Wes!

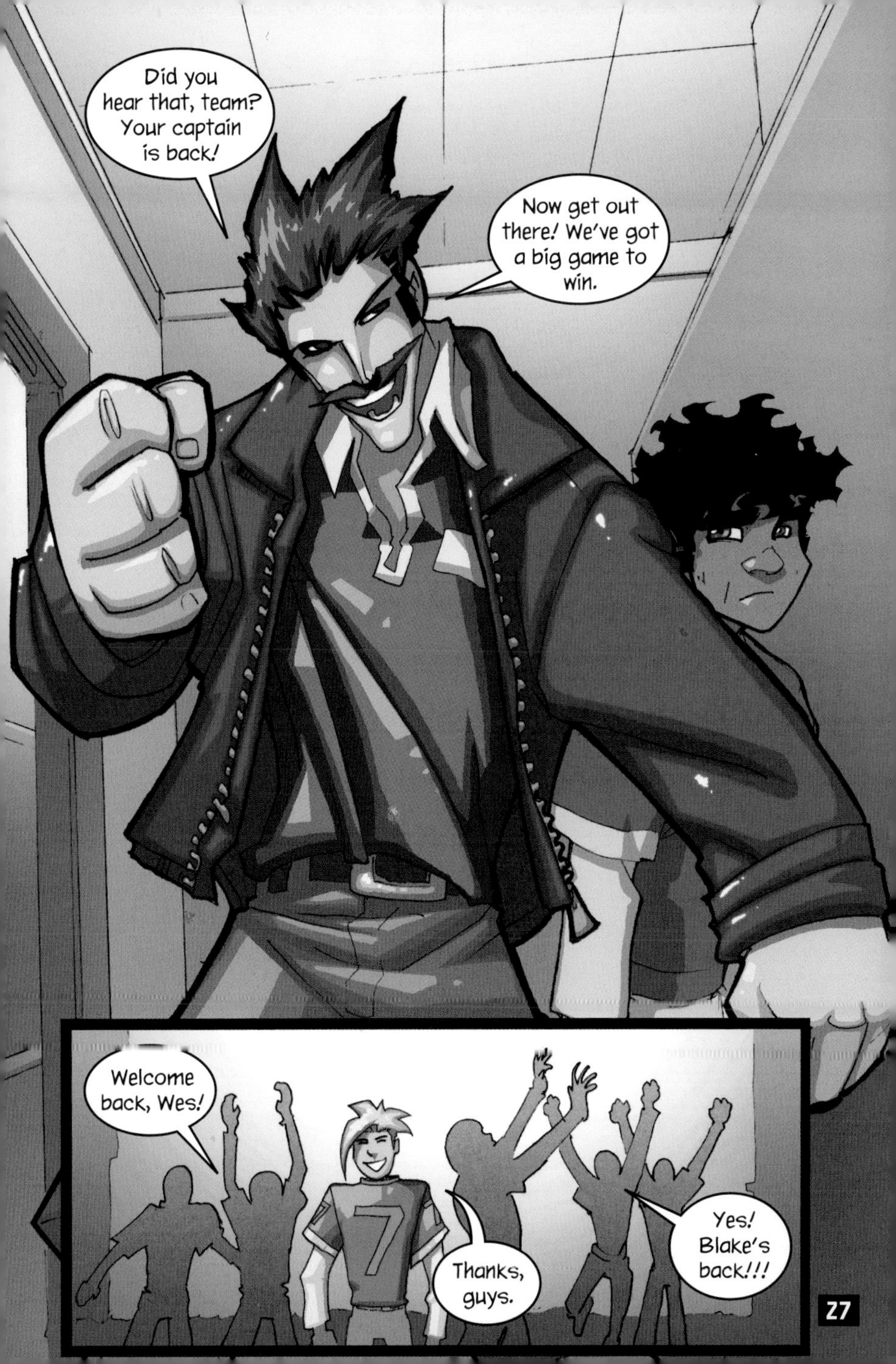
Did you hear that, team? Your captain is back!
Now get out there! We've got a big game to win.
Welcome back, Wes!
Thanks, guys.
Yes! Blake's back!!!

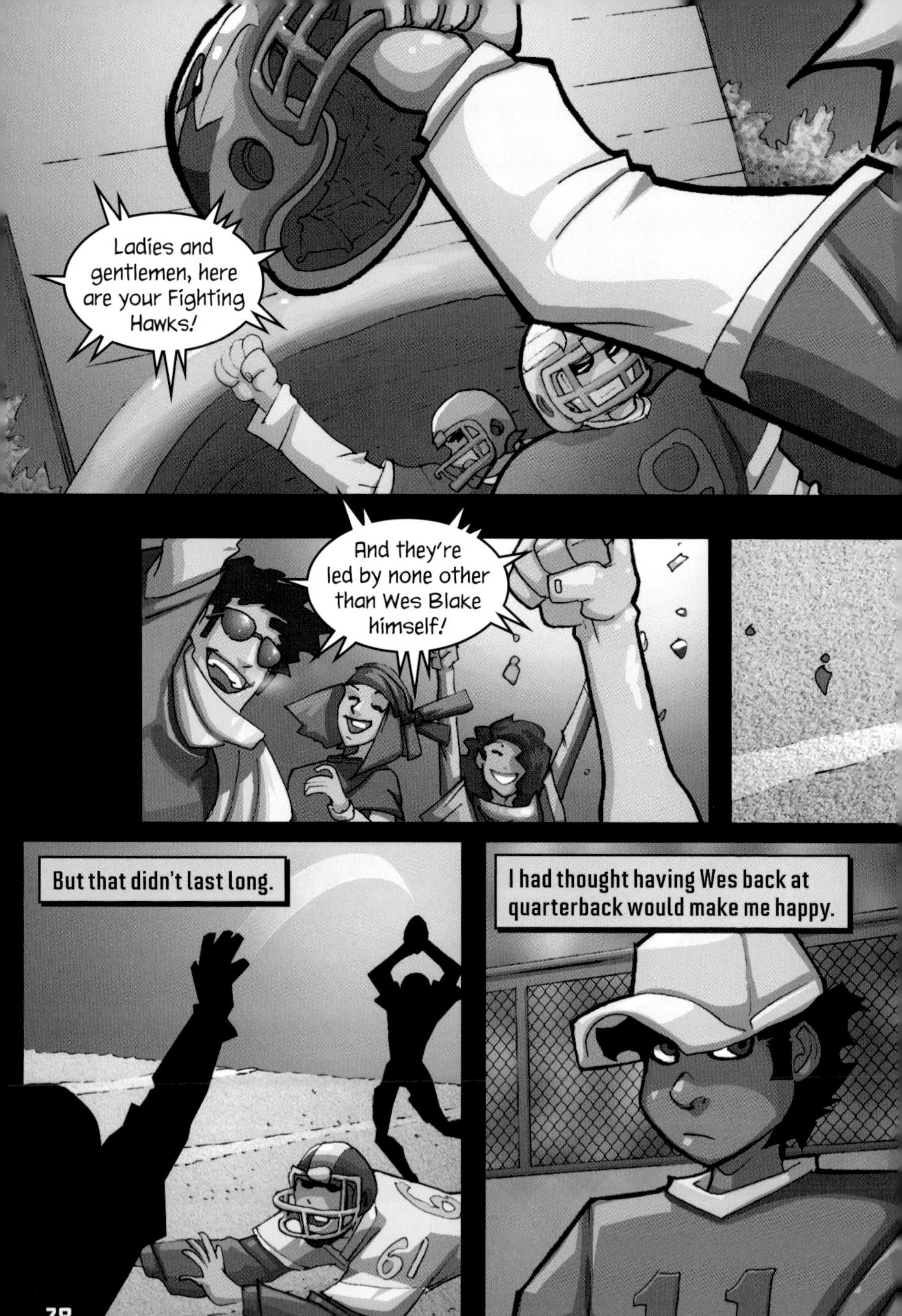
Ladies and gentlemen, here are your Fighting Hawks!
And they're led by none other than Wes Blake himself!
But that didn't last long.
I had thought having Wes back at quarterback would make me happy.
61
11

Wes was kind of rusty at first.

BOINK

But actually, it felt kinda weird being back on the sidelines.

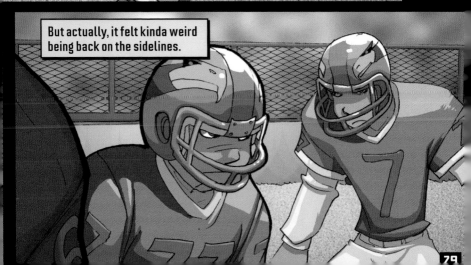

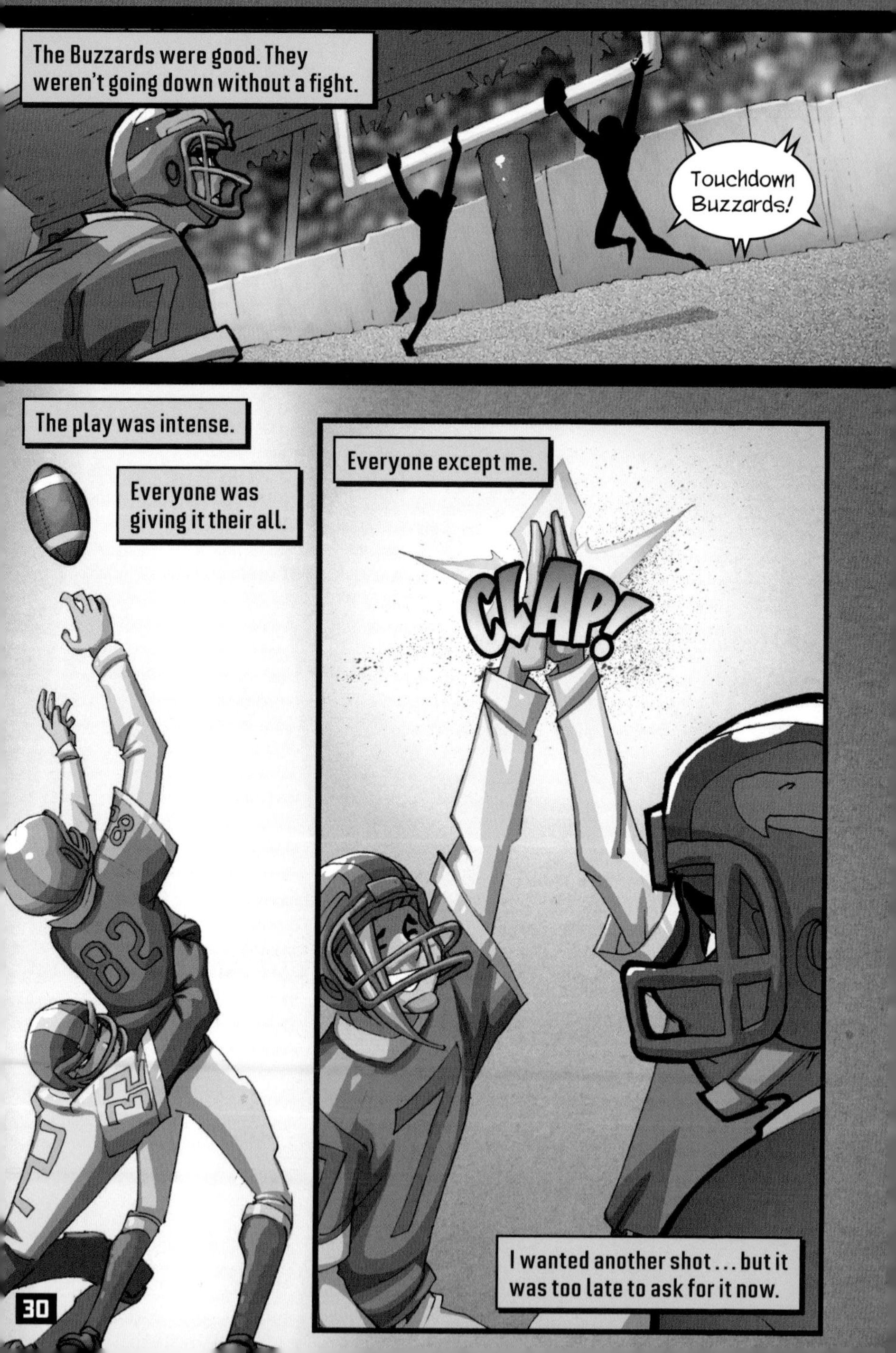
The Buzzards were good. They weren't going down without a fight.
Touchdown Buzzards!
The play was intense.
Everyone was giving it their all.
Everyone except me.
CLAP!
I wanted another shot . . . but it was too late to ask for it now.

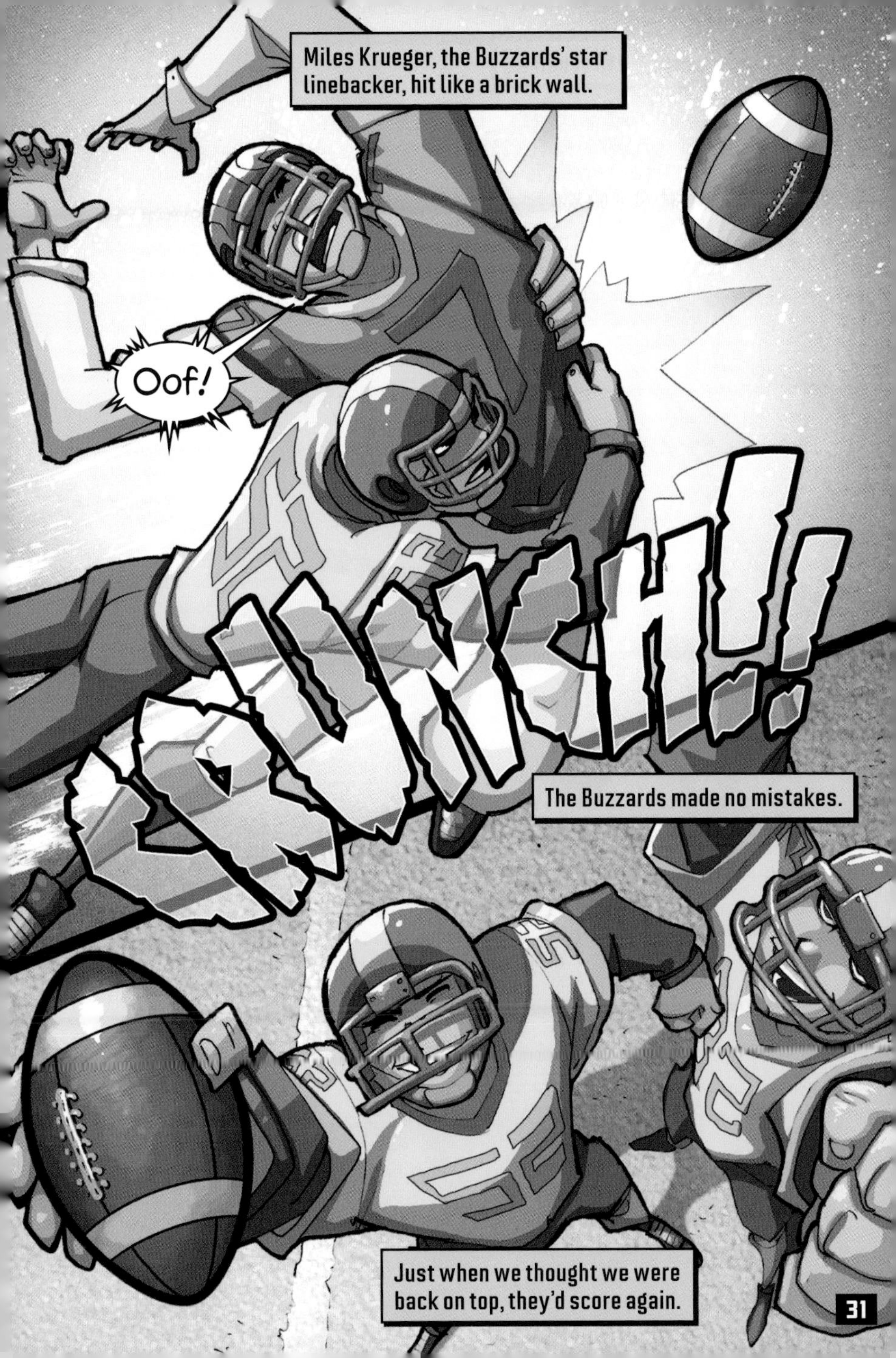
Miles Krueger, the Buzzards' star linebacker, hit like a brick wall.
Oof!
CRUNCH!!
The Buzzards made no mistakes.
Just when we thought we were back on top, they'd score again.

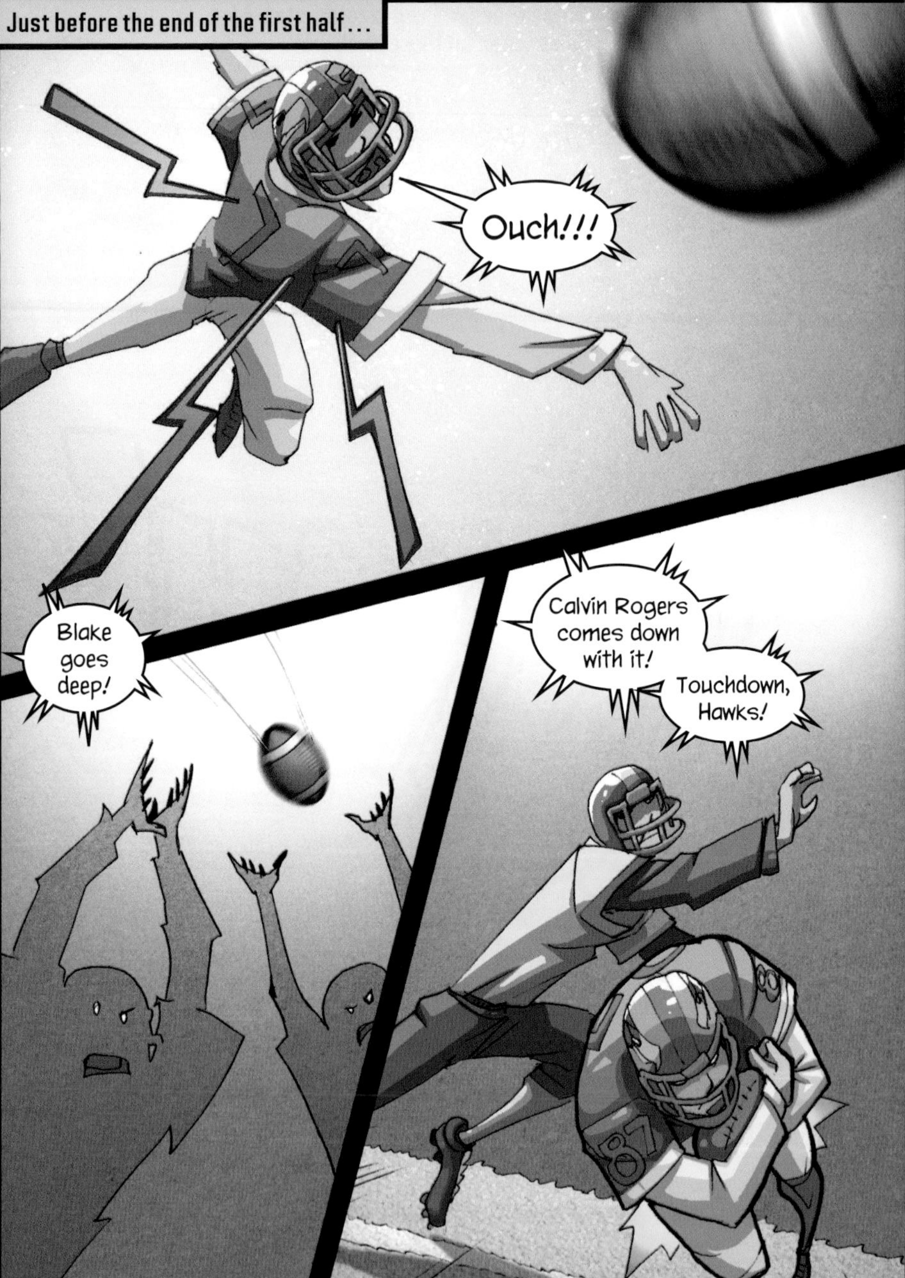
Just before the end of the first half . . .
Ouch!!!
Blake goes deep!
Calvin Rogers comes down with it!
Touchdown, Hawks!

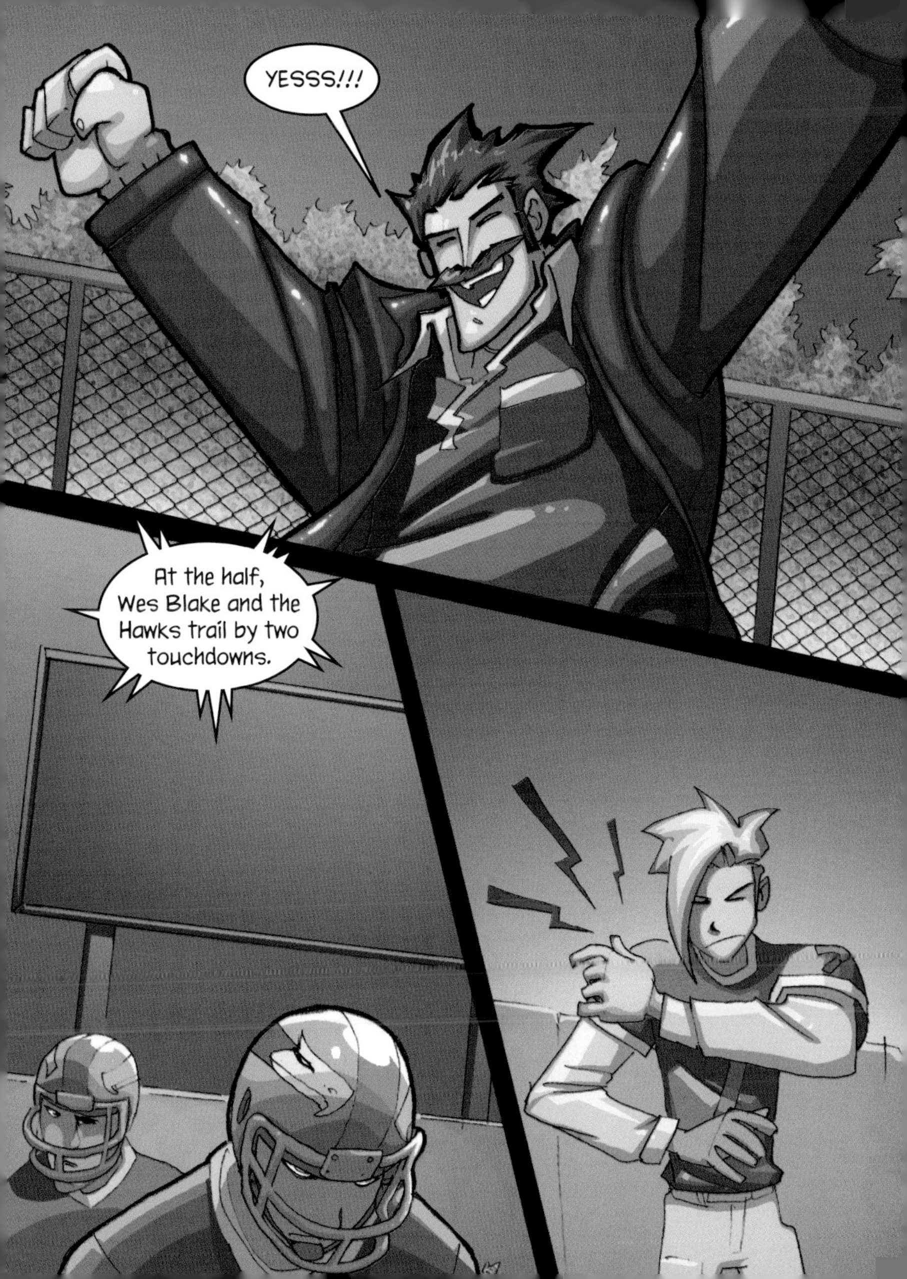
YESSS!!!
At the half, Wes Blake and the Hawks trail by two touchdowns.

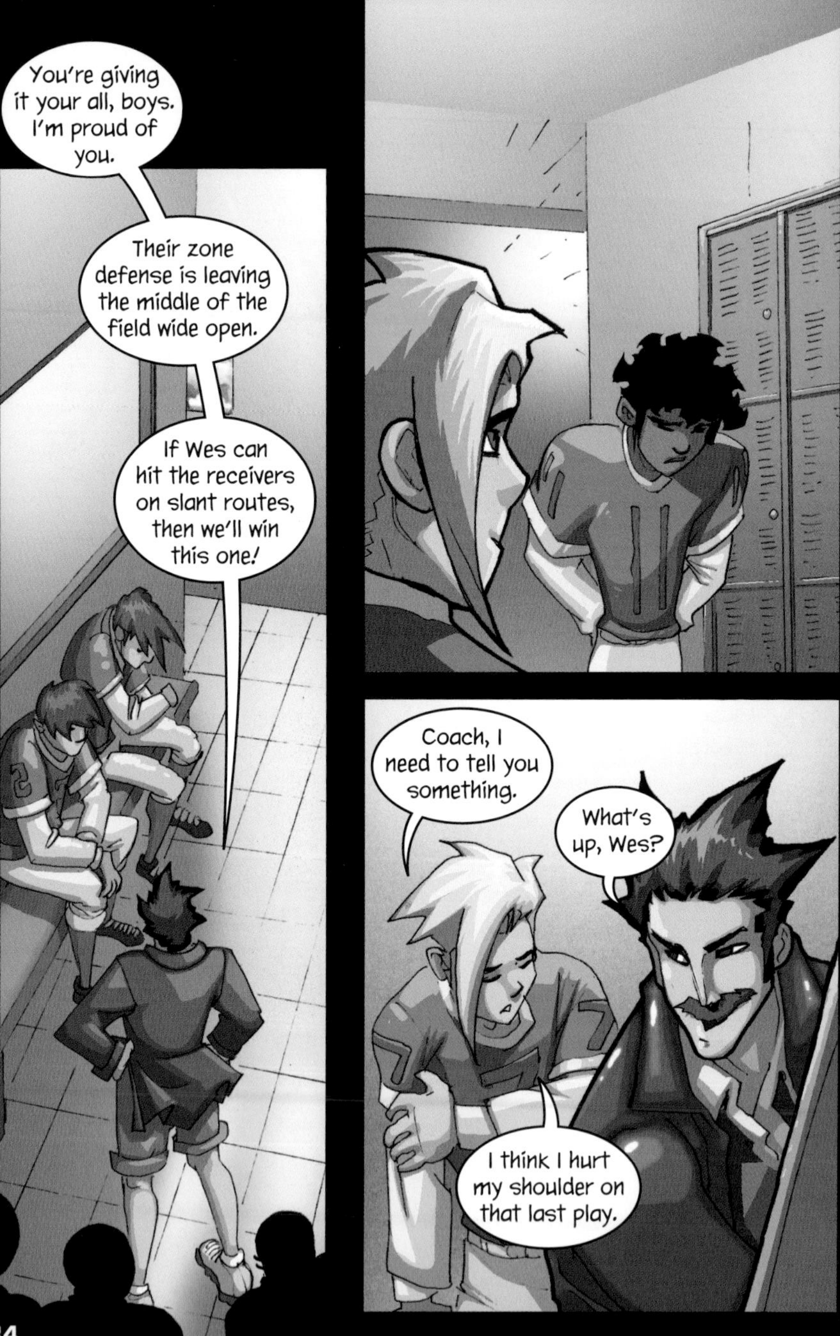
You're giving it your all, boys. I'm proud of you.
Their zone defense is leaving the middle of the field wide open.
If Wes can hit the receivers on slant routes, then we'll win this one!
Coach, I need to tell you something.
What's up, Wes?
I think I hurt my shoulder on that last play.

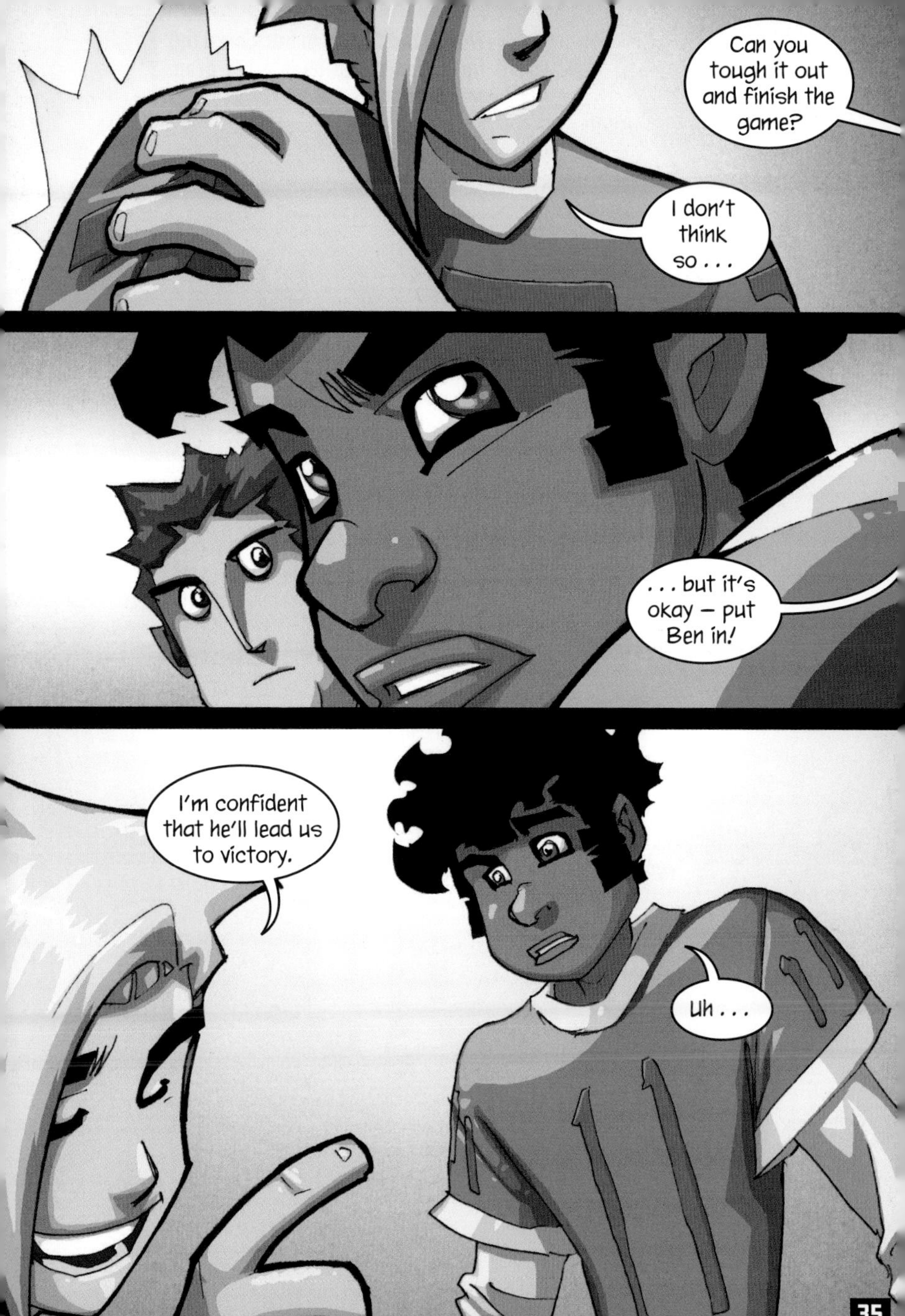
Can you tough it out and finish the game?
I don't think so . . .
. . . but it's okay – put Ben in!
I'm confident that he'll lead us to victory.
Uh . . .

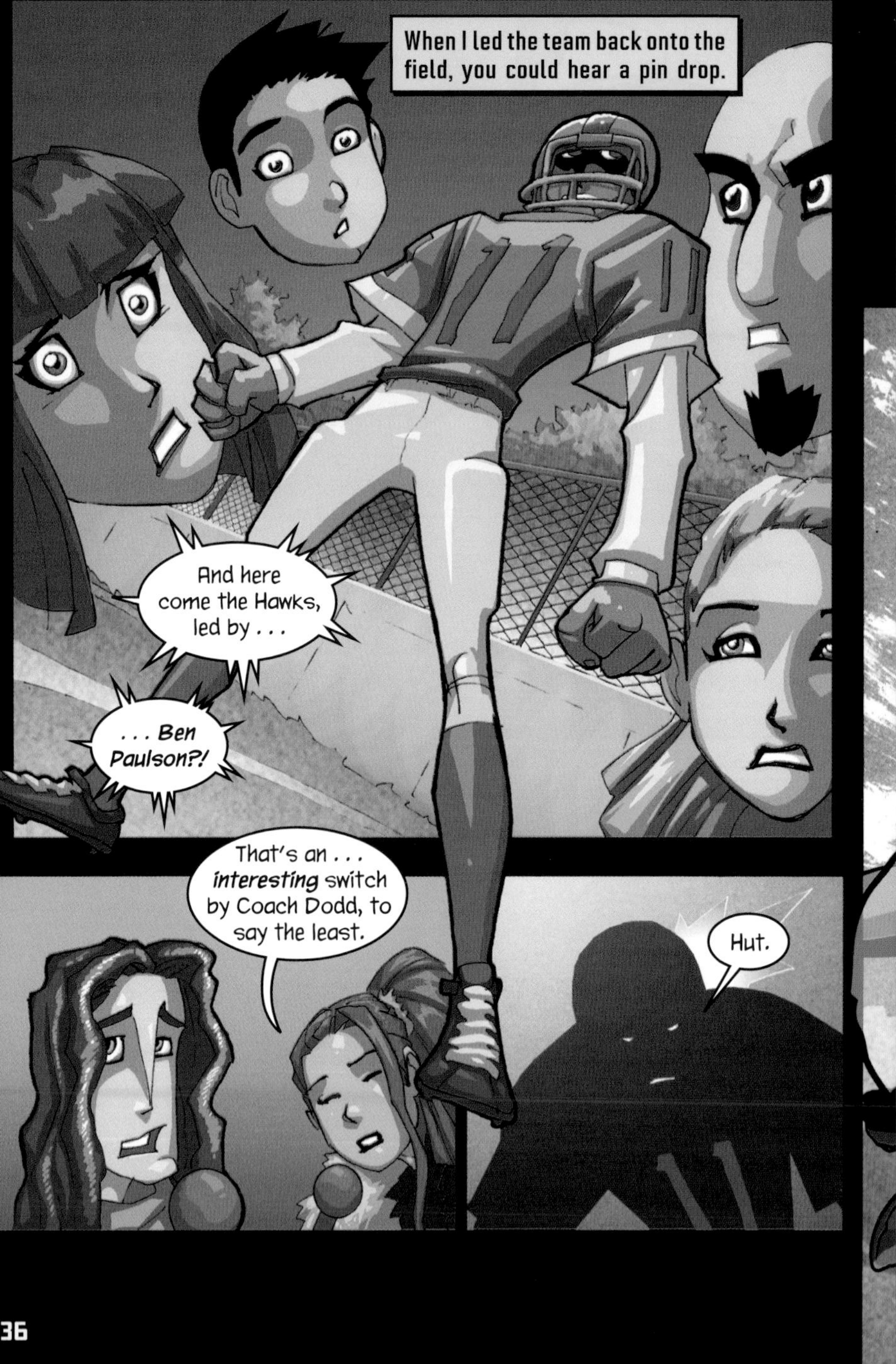
When I led the team back onto the field, you could hear a pin drop.
And here come the Hawks, led by . . .
. . . Ben Paulson?!
That's an . . . interesting switch by Coach Dodd, to say the least.
Hut.

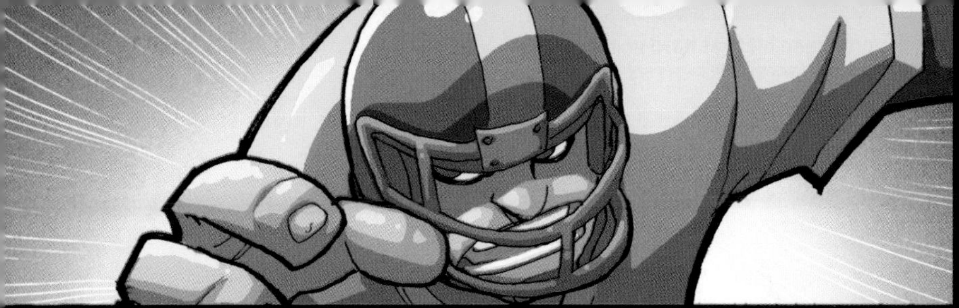

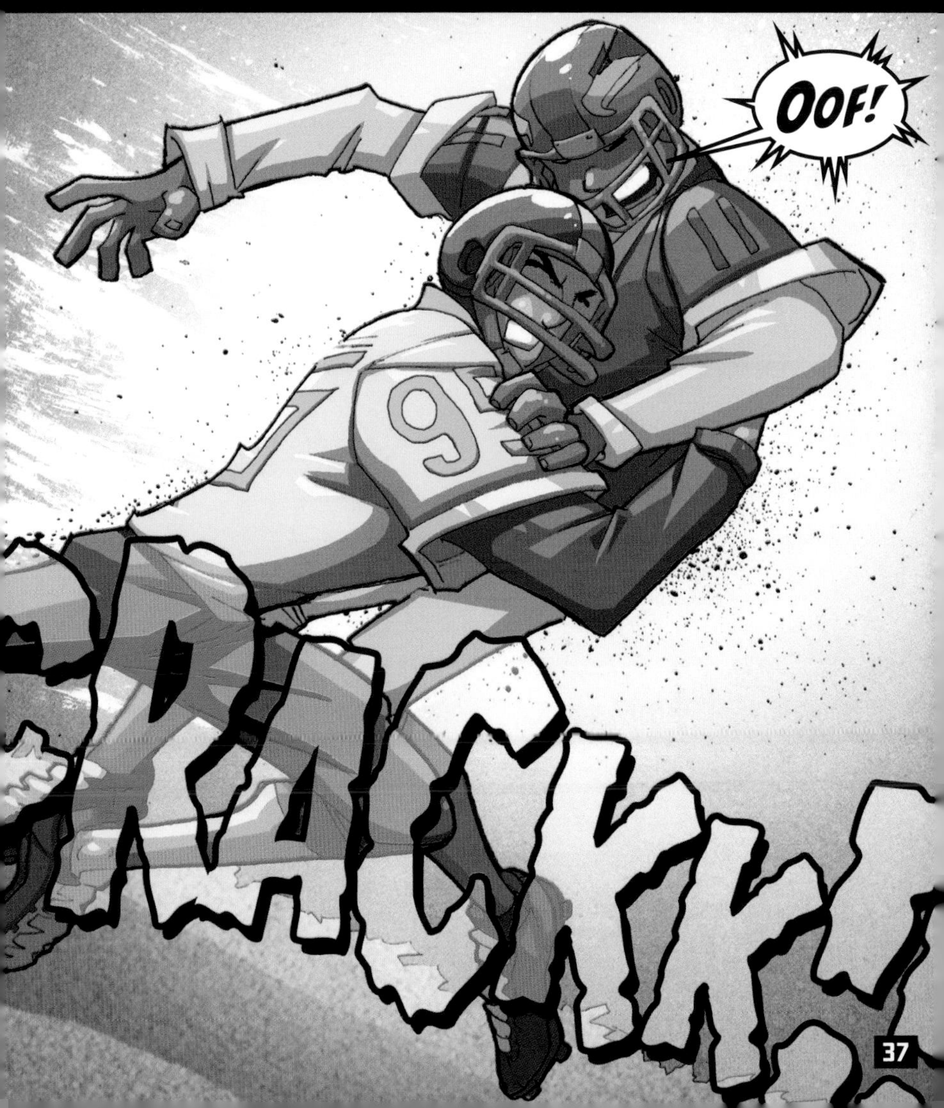
OOF!

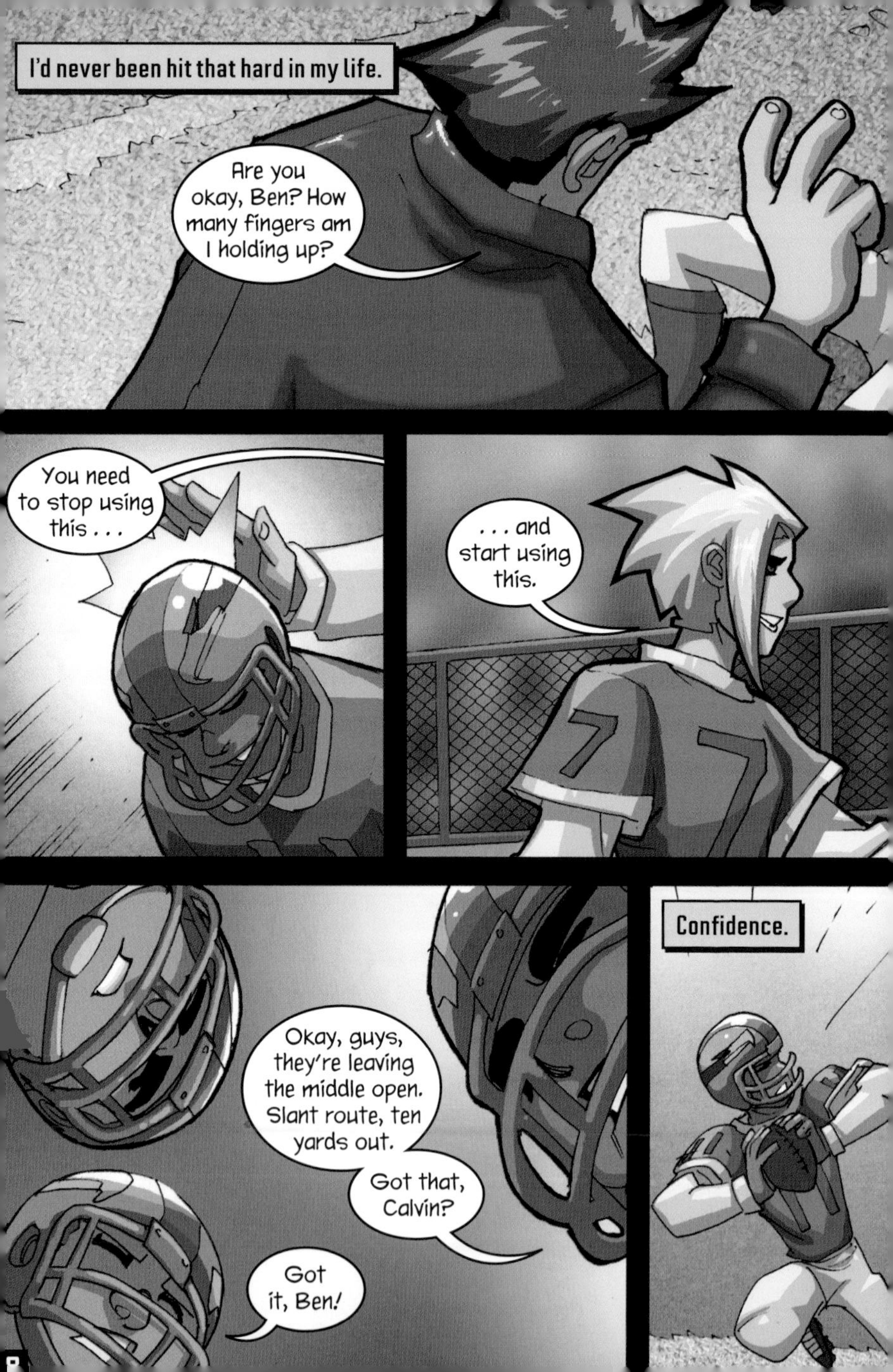
I'd never been hit that hard in my life.
Are you okay, Ben? How many fingers am I holding up?
You need to stop using this . . .
. . . and start using this.
Confidence.
Okay, guys, they're leaving the middle open. Slant route, ten yards out.
Got that, Calvin?
Got it, Ben!

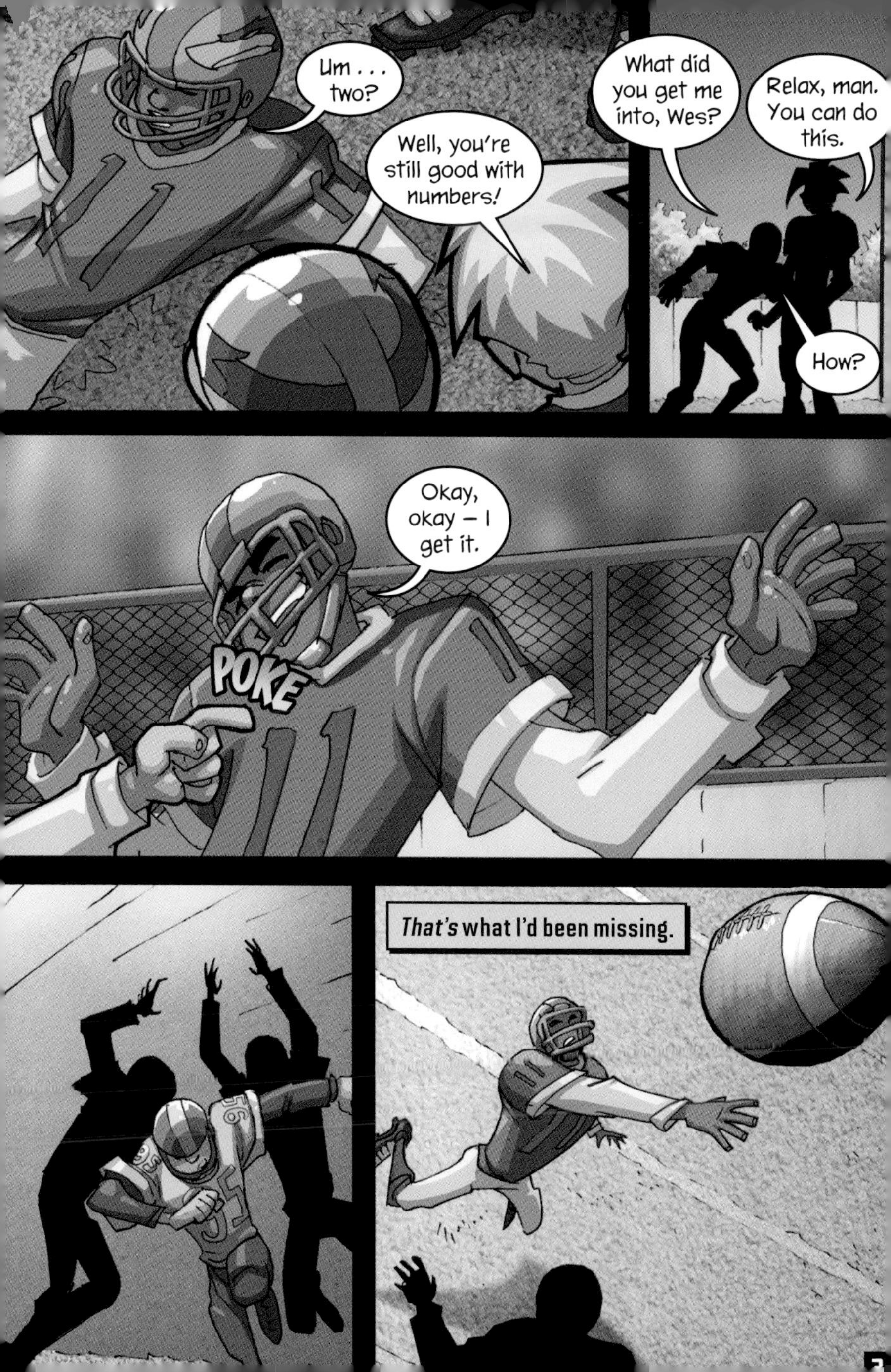
Um . . . two?
Well, you're still good with numbers!
What did you get me into, Wes?
Relax, man. You can do this.
How?
Okay, okay — I get it.
POKE
That's what I'd been missing.

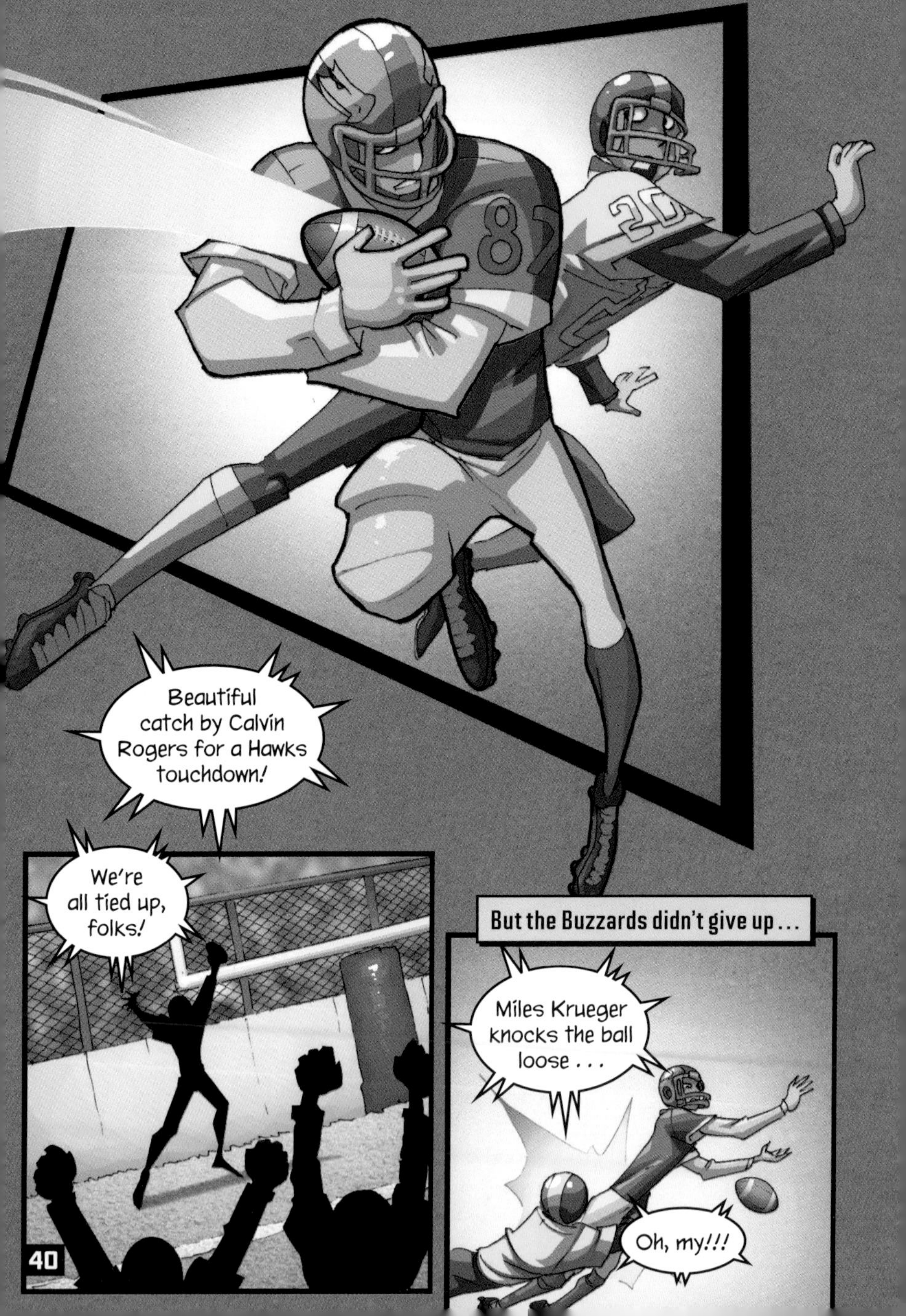
Beautiful catch by Calvin Rogers for a Hawks touchdown!
We're all tied up, folks!
But the Buzzards didn't give up . . .
Miles Krueger knocks the ball loose . . .
Oh, my!!!

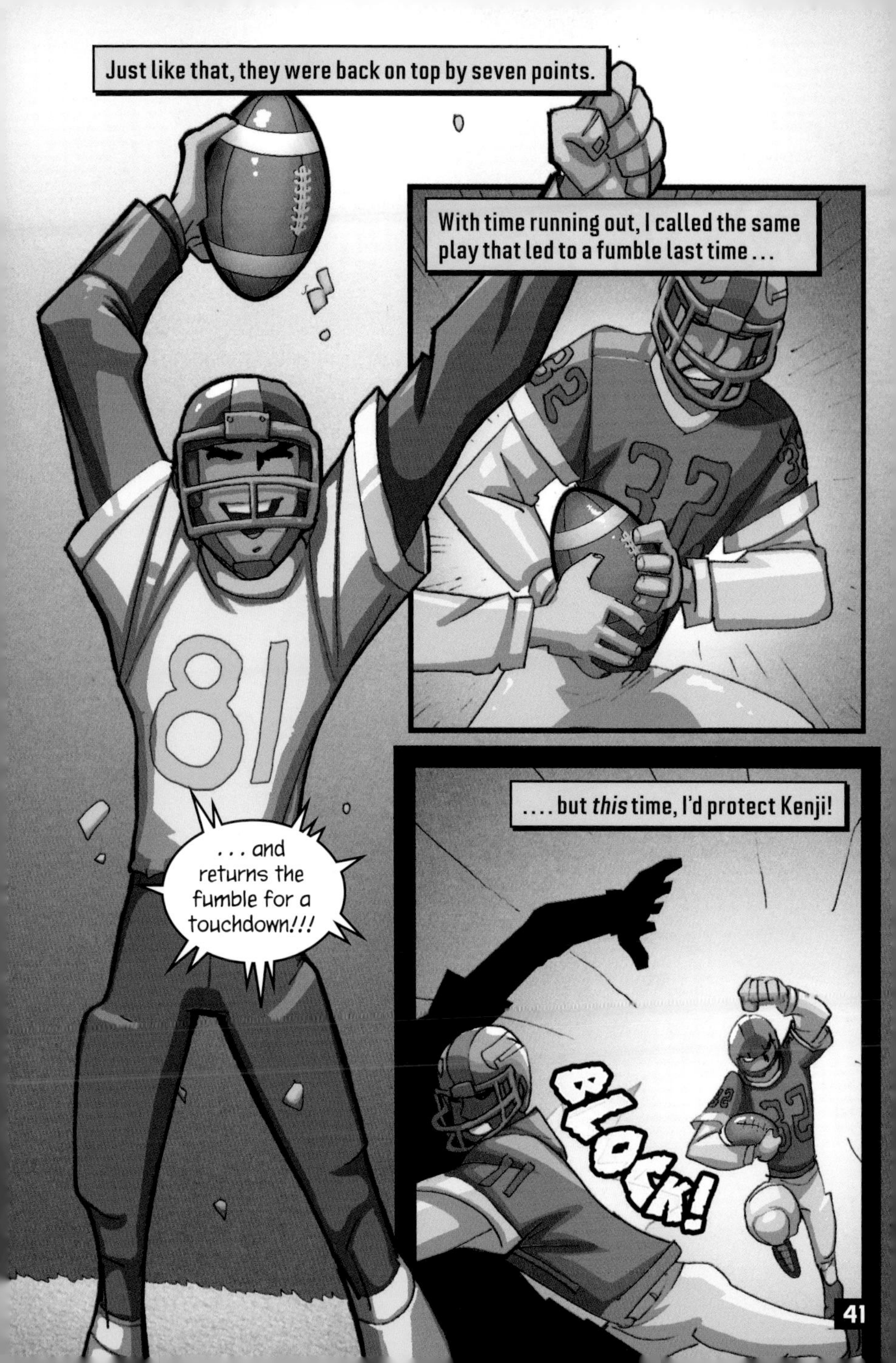
Just like that, they were back on top by seven points.
. . . and returns the fumble for a touchdown!!!
With time running out, I called the same play that led to a fumble last time . . .
. . . . but *this* time, I'd protect Kenji!
BLOCK!

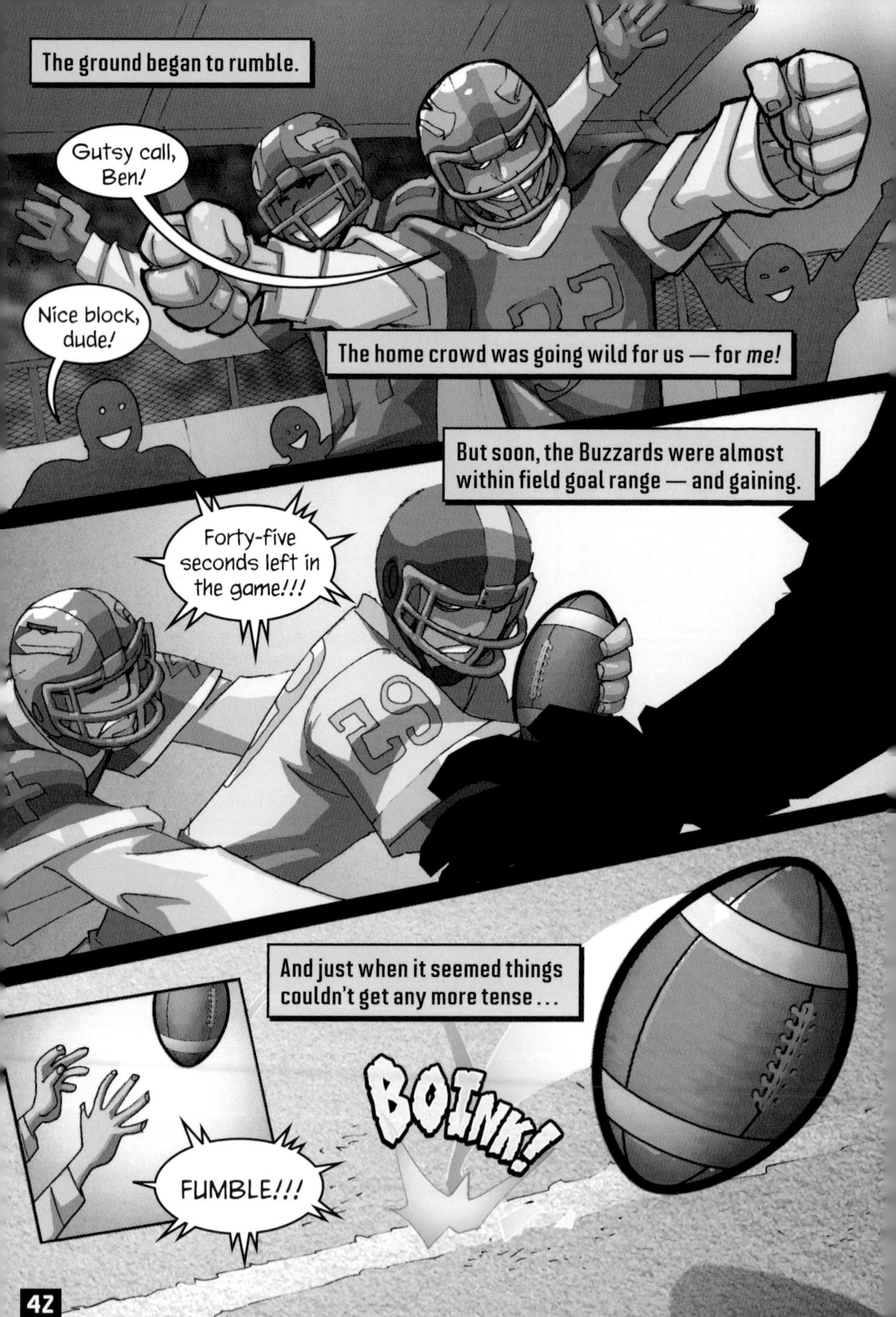

The ground began to rumble.
Gutsy call, Ben!
Nice block, dude!
The home crowd was going wild for us — for *me!*
But soon, the Buzzards were almost within field goal range — and gaining.
Forty-five seconds left in the game!!!
And just when it seemed things couldn't get any more tense . . .
BOINK!
FUMBLE!!!

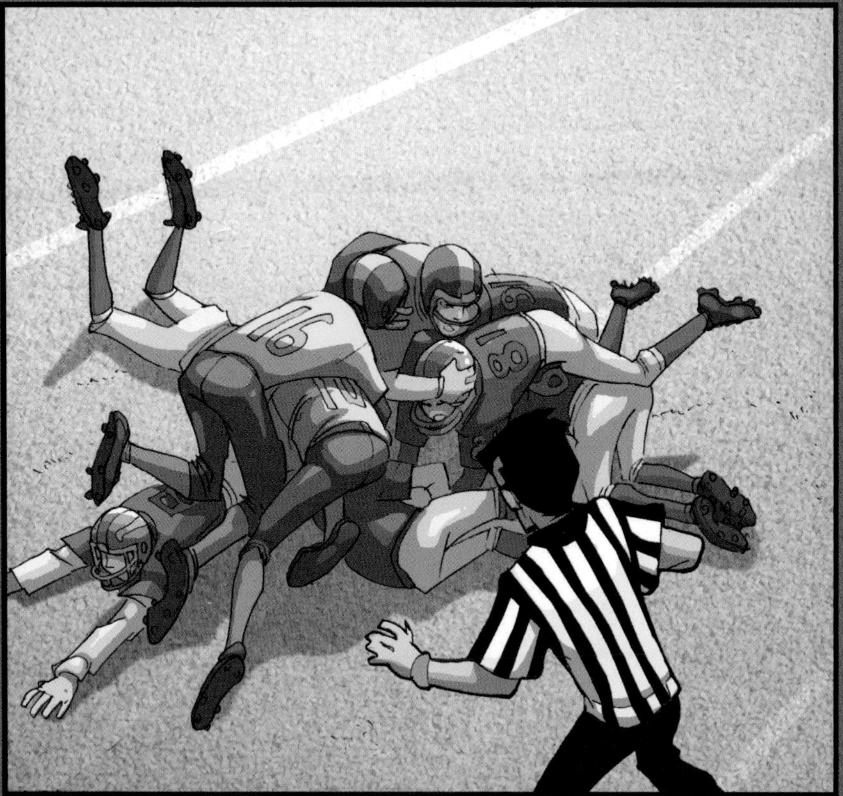

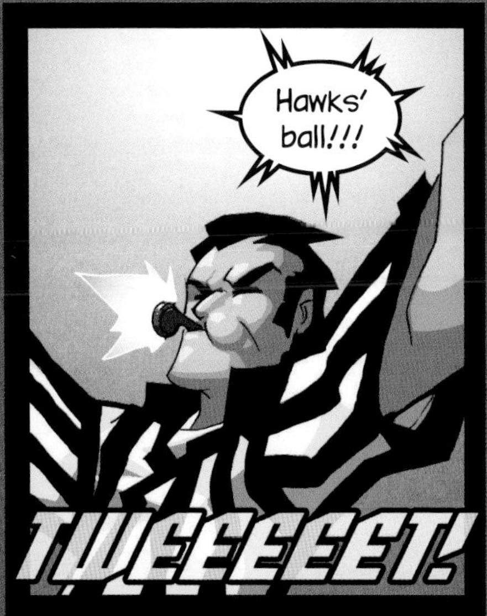
Hawks' ball!!!
TWEEEEEET!

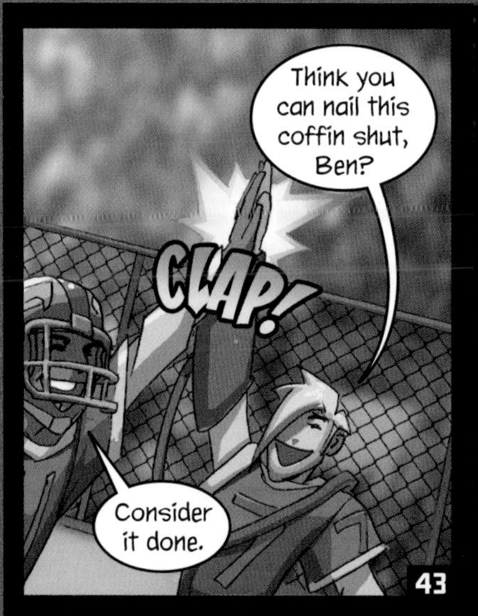
Think you can nail this coffin shut, Ben?
CLAP!
Consider it done.

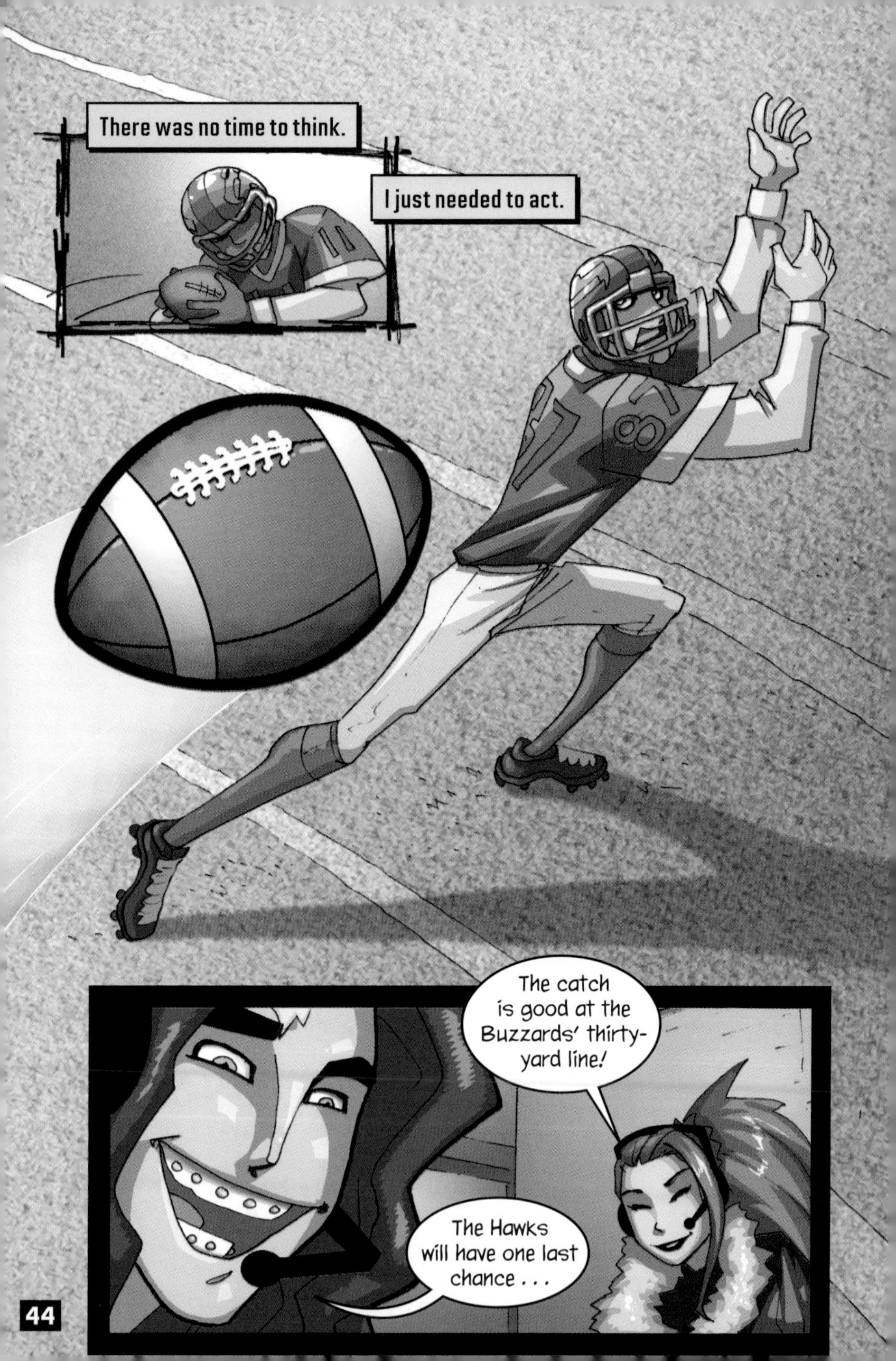
There was no time to think.
I just needed to act.
The catch is good at the Buzzards' thirty-yard line!
The Hawks will have one last chance . . .

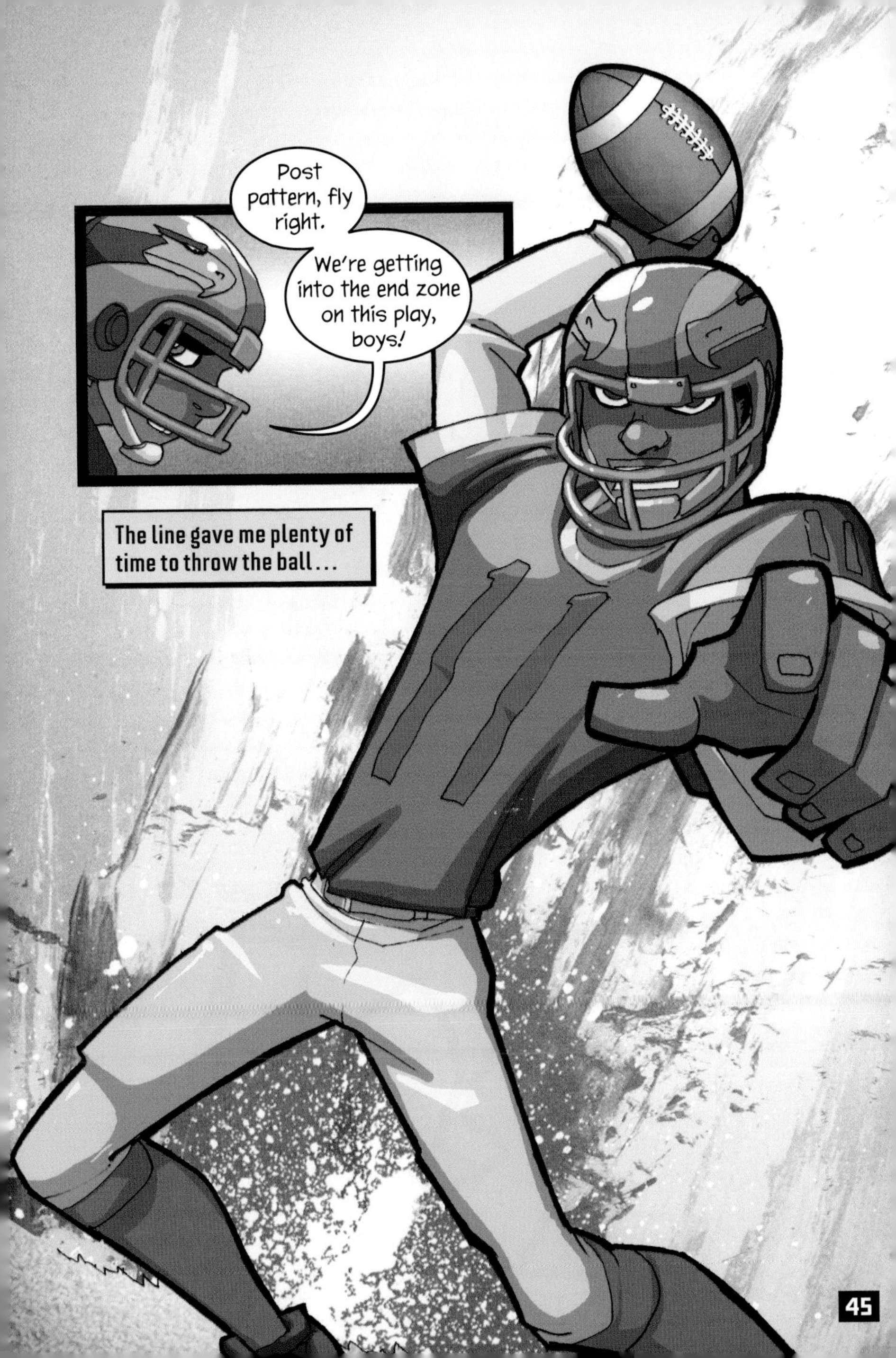
Post pattern, fly right.
We're getting into the end zone on this play, boys!
The line gave me plenty of time to throw the ball . . .

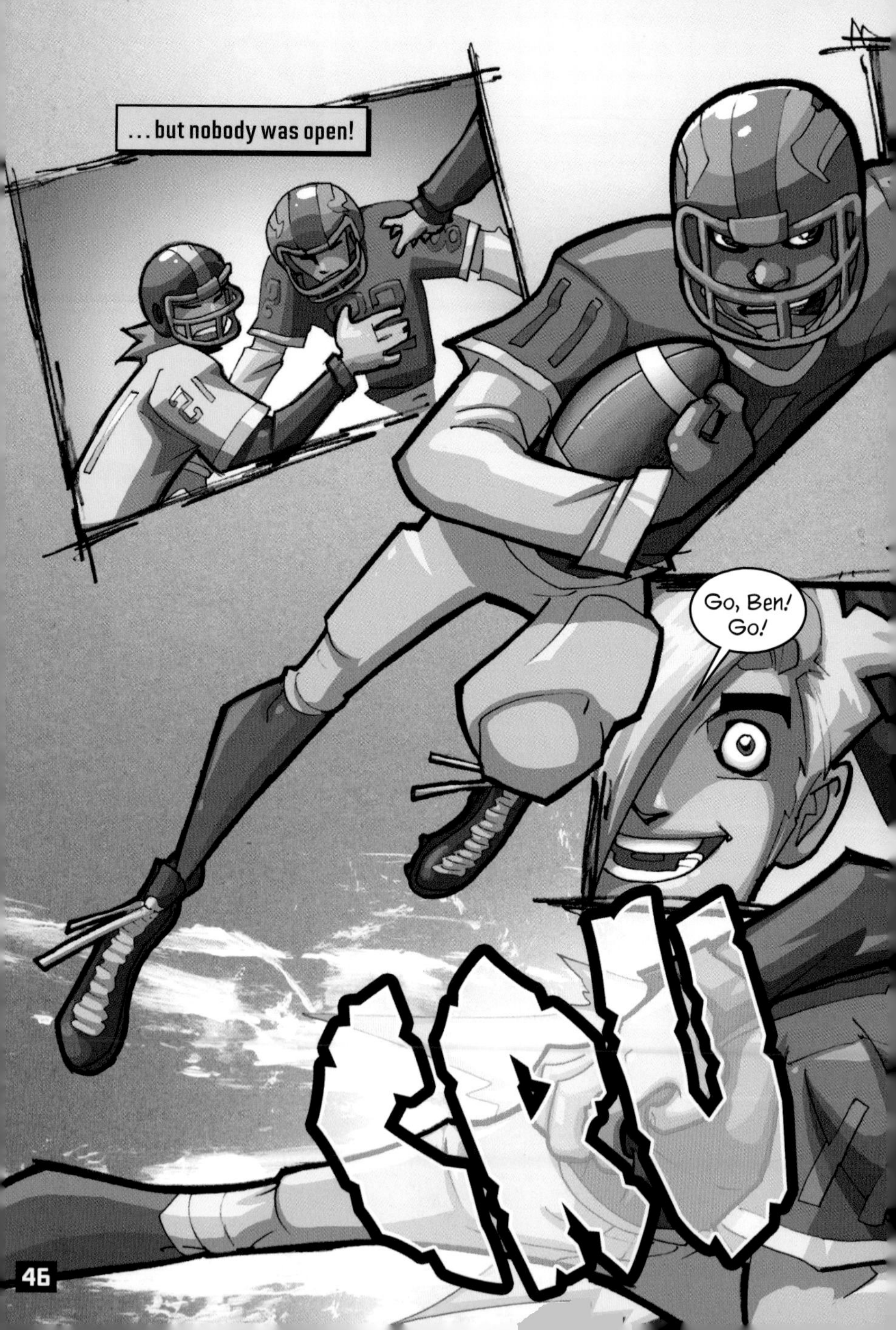
. . . but nobody was open!
Go, Ben! Go!

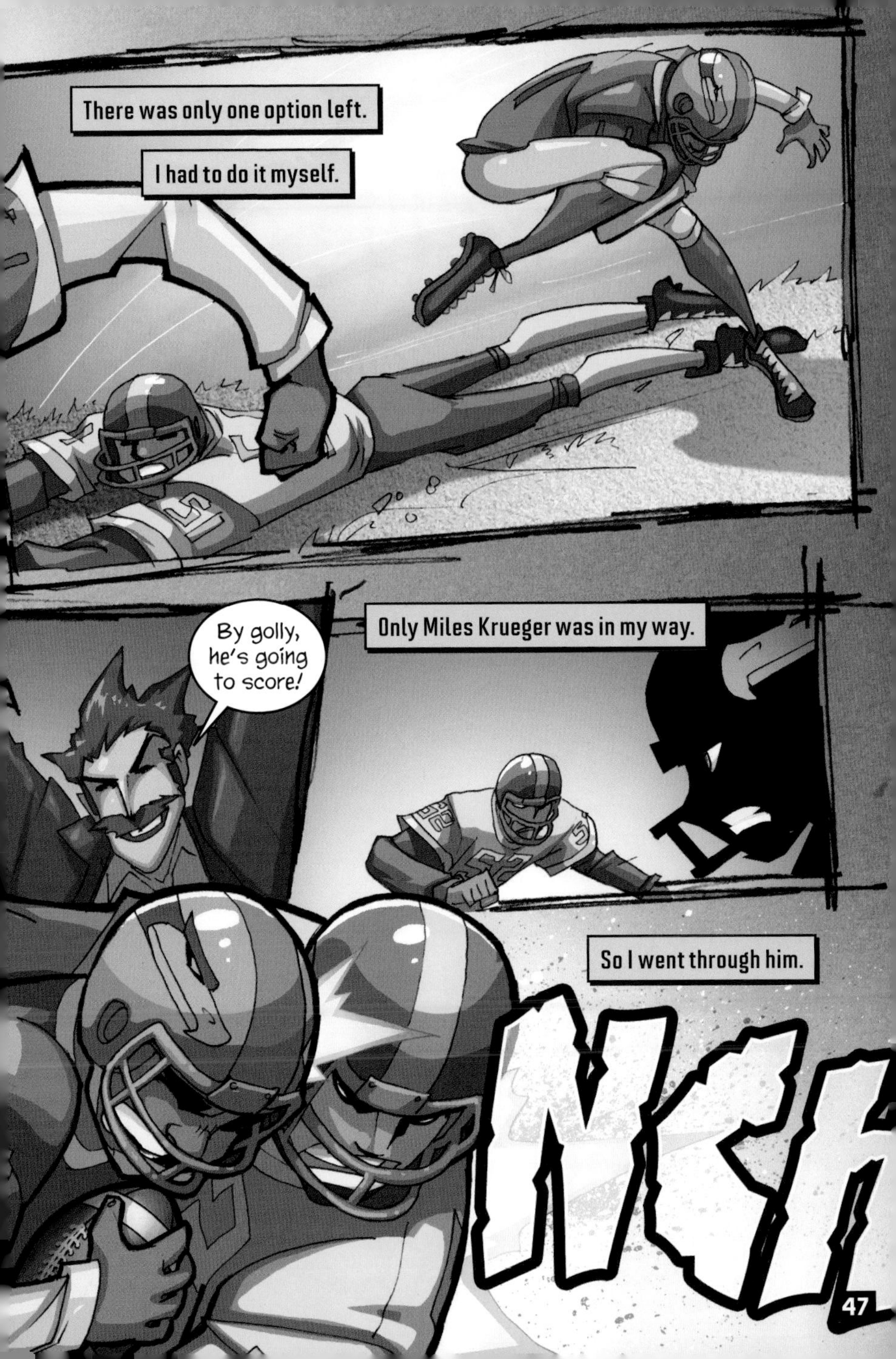
There was only one option left.
I had to do it myself.
Only Miles Krueger was in my way.
By golly, he's going to score!
So I went through him.

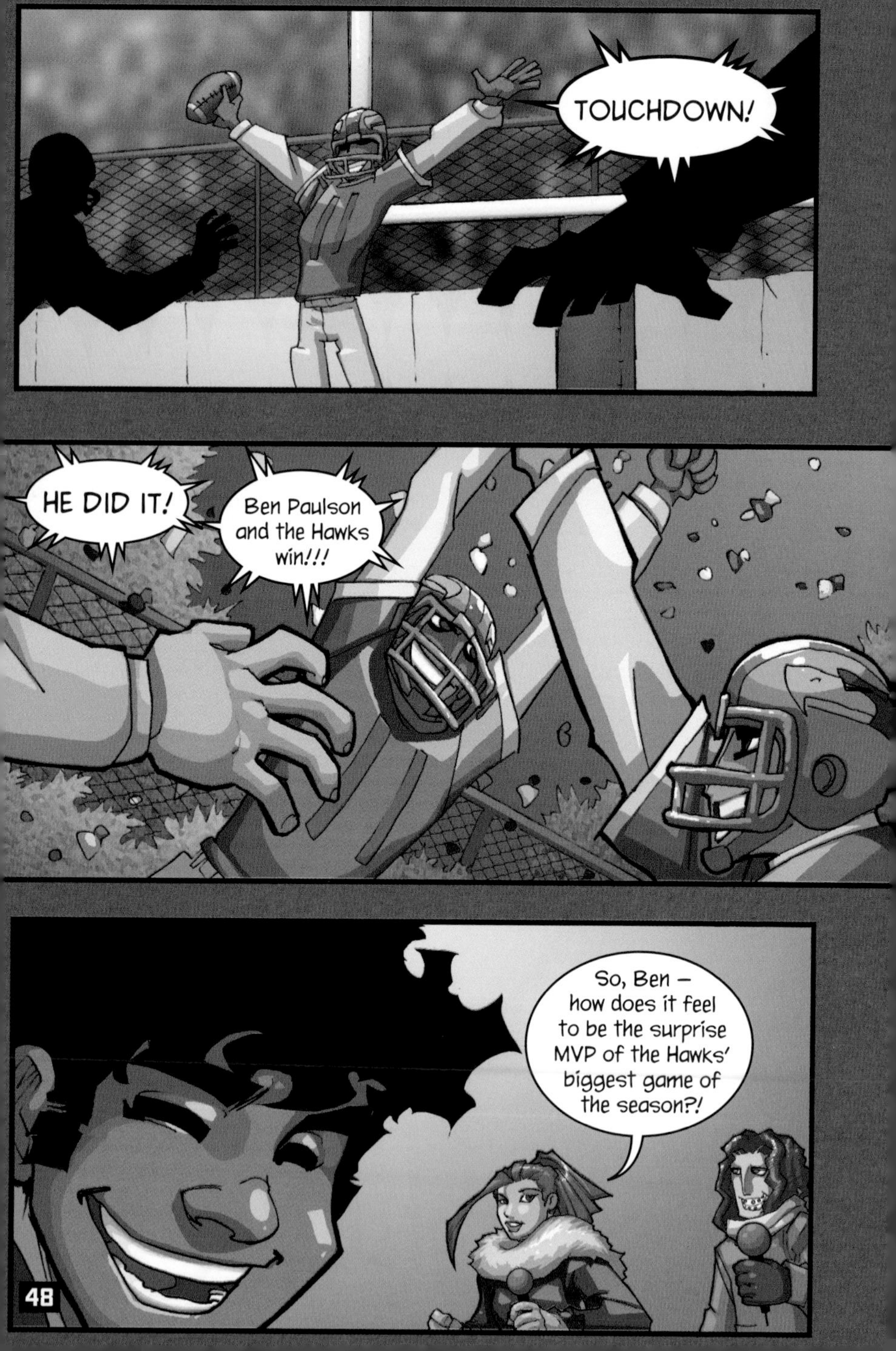
TOUCHDOWN!
HE DID IT!
Ben Paulson and the Hawks win!!!
So, Ben — how does it feel to be the surprise MVP of the Hawks' biggest game of the season?!

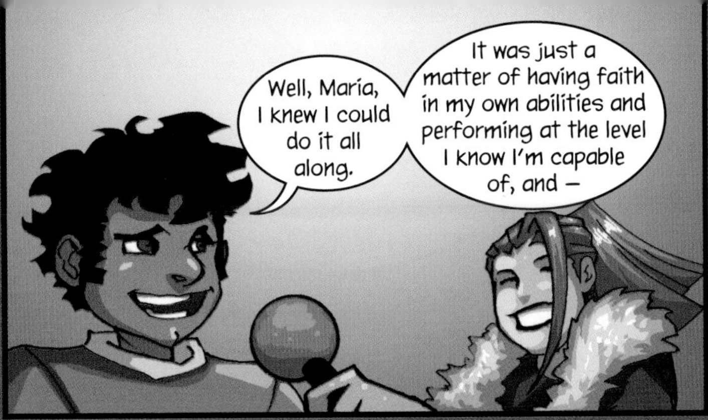
Well, Maria, I knew I could do it all along.
It was just a matter of having faith in my own abilities and performing at the level I know I'm capable of, and —

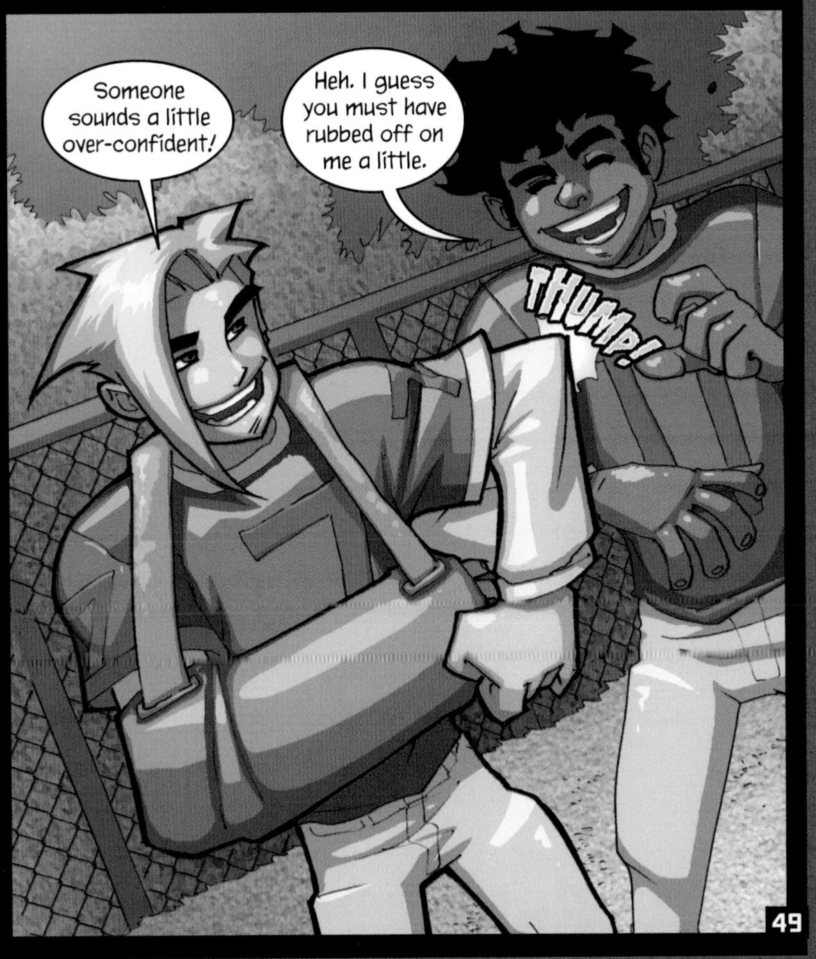
Someone sounds a little over-confident!
Heh. I guess you must have rubbed off on me a little.
THUMP!

SPORTS ZONE
POSTGAME RECAP

FBL
FOOTBALL

PNT
PAINTBALL

SOC
SOCCER

BSL
BASEBALL

BBL
BASKETBALL

HKY
HOCKEY

BEN PAULSON SURPRISES EVERYONE IN HAWKS' BIG WIN!

BY THE NUMBERS

STATS LEADERS:
TDs: PAULSON, 3
SACKS: KRUEGER, 4

STORY: Everyone was panicking when Wes Blake went down with an injured shoulder in the big game against the Buzzards. But when Ben Paulson stepped up, he shocked everyone by throwing multiple touchdowns and leading the Hawks to a come-from-behind victory. When asked how it felt, Ben said, "It was great to lead the team to a win — but I couldn't have done it without Wes Blake's help."

Sports Illustrated KIDS

UP NEXT: SI KIDS INFO CENTER

BLZ vs BKS 3-1
TGR vs RDR 33-32
EAG vs BAN 14-7
SPA vs WLD 4-3
BAN vs RDR 21-15
RZR vs LIG 4-3

SZ POSTGAME EXTRA

WHERE ***YOU*** ANALYZE THE GAME!

Football fans got a real treat today when the Hawks faced off against the Buzzards in a memorable gridiron battle. Let's go into the stands and ask some fans for their opinions on the day's big game . . .

DISCUSSION QUESTION 1

Which quarterback do you like more — Ben Paulson or Wes Blake? Why?

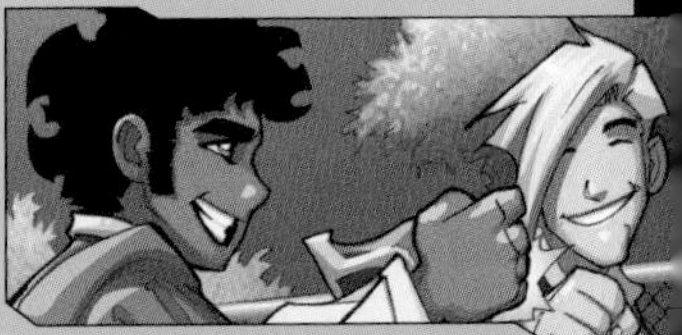

DISCUSSION QUESTION 2

Do you play football? What's your favorite position? Which position is the hardest to play? Talk about football.

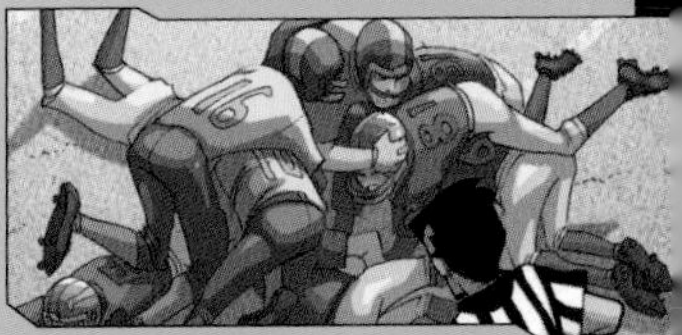

WRITING PROMPT 1

Wes and Ben helped each other out. Who have you helped? Who has helped you? What happened? Write about your helpful experiences.

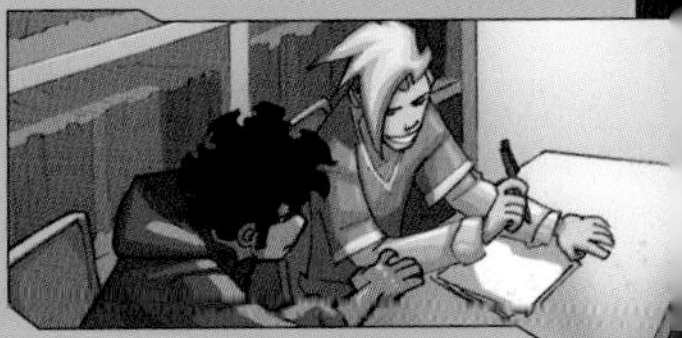

WRITING PROMPT 2

Ben thinks confidence is important. What kinds of things are you confident about? What aren't you confident about? Write about it!

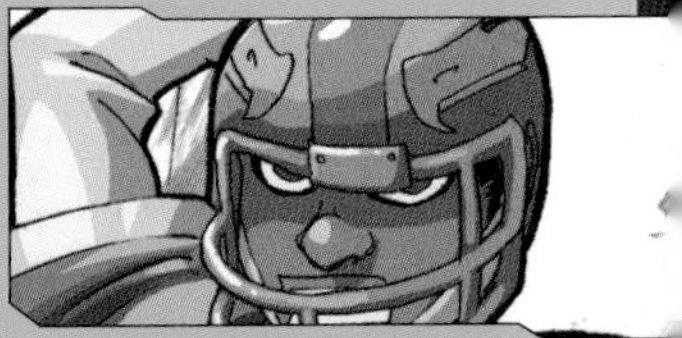

GLOSSARY

BLITZ (BLITS)—a play where the defense tries to tackle the quarterback right after the snap

CERTIFIED (SUR-tuh-fied)—guaranteed to be genuine or real

CONFIDENT (KON-fuh-duhnt)—having a strong belief in yourself

EPIC (EP-ik)—heroic or impressive

HAZY (HAYZ-ee)—unclear or out of focus

HESITATING (HEZ-uh-tate-ing)—pausing before doing something due to uncertainty

INTENSE (in-TENSS)—very strong or overwhelming

PRESSURE (PRESH-ur)—strong influence or strain

PUNCH LINE (PUHNCH LINE)—the part of the joke that makes people laugh

SLANT ROUTE (SLANT ROUT)—a pattern run by a receiver where the receiver runs up the field at about a 45-degree angle

CREATORS

Brandon Terrell › *Author*

Brandon Terrell is a writer and filmmaker who has worked in the Minnesota film and television community for nearly ten years. He is the author of the graphic novel *Horrorwood*, published by Ape Entertainment. He is also an avid baseball fan, and is crazy about the Minnesota Twins. Terrell lives in Saint Paul with his wife, Jennifer.

Gerardo Sandoval › *Illustrator*

Gerardo Sandoval is a professional comic book illustrator from Mexico. He has worked on many well-known comics including Tomb Raider books from Top Cow Production. He has also worked on designs for posters and card sets.

Benny Fuentes › *Colorist*

Benny Fuentes lives in Villahermosa, Tabasco in Mexico, where the temperature is just as hot as the sauce. He studied graphic design in college, but now he works as a full-time colorist in the comic book and graphic novel industry for companies like Marvel, DC Comics, and Top Cow Productions. He shares his home with two crazy cats, Chelo and Kitty, who act like they own the place.

Sports Illustrated KIDS
GRAPHIC NOVELS
QUICK COMIC

TOU YANG IN:
KICKOFF BLITZ

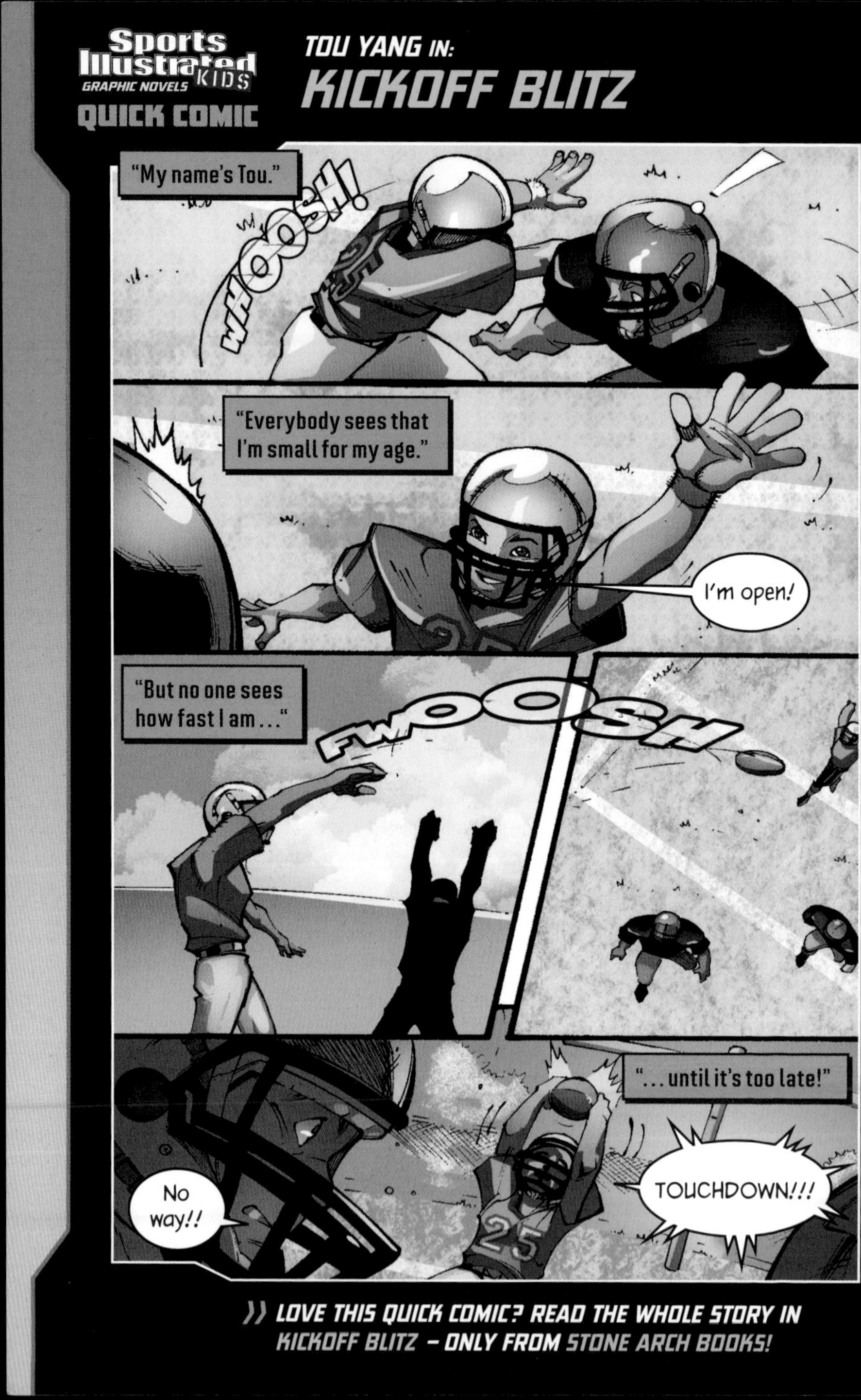

"My name's Tou."
WHOOSH!
"Everybody sees that I'm small for my age."
I'm open!
"But no one sees how fast I am..."
FWOOOSH
"...until it's too late!"
No way!!
TOUCHDOWN!!!

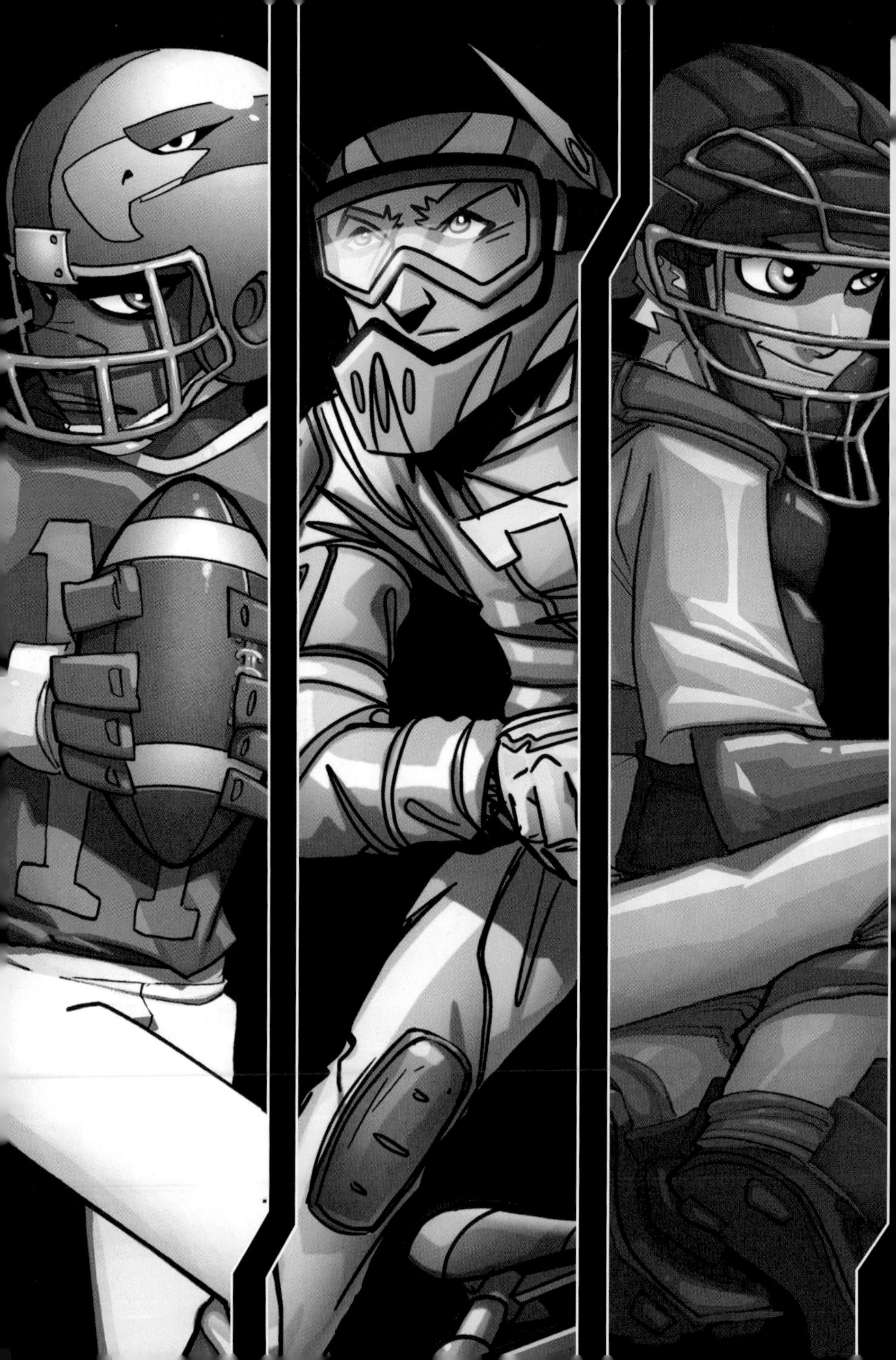

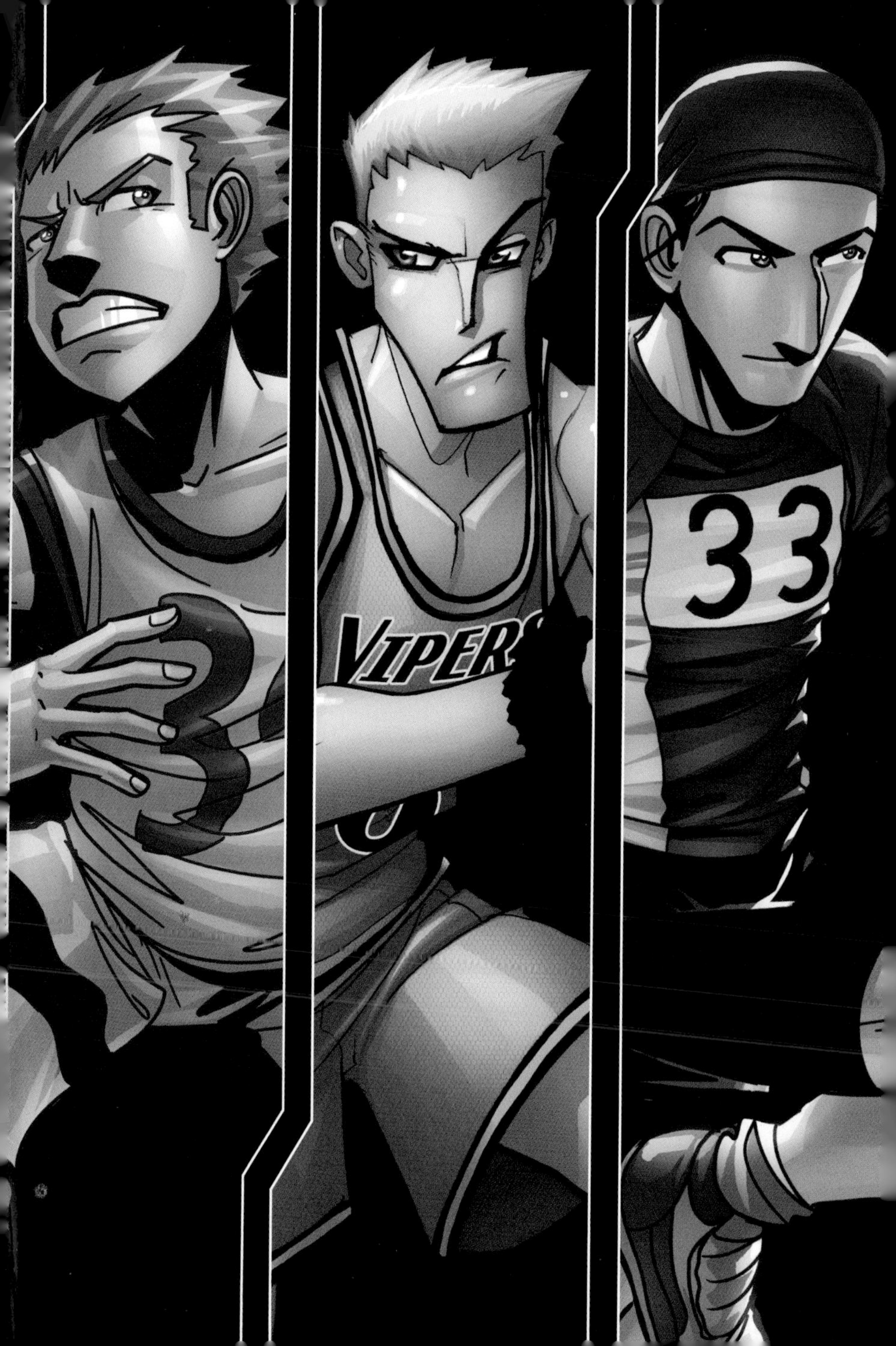
VIPERS
33

Sports Illustrated KIDS

GRAPHIC NOVELS

STONE ARCH BOOKS
a capstone imprint